MIRIAM'S JANUARY PROMISE

AN AMISH ROMANCE BIRTHDAY SERIES

TRACY FREDRYCHOWSKI

Published in South Carolina by The Tracer Group, LLC

https://tracyfredrychowski.com

THE HOLY BIBLE, NEW INTERNATIONAL VERSION®, NIV®
Copyright © 1973, 1978, 1984, 2011 by Biblica, Inc.™ Used by permission. All rights reserved worldwide.

ISBN: 979-8-9996193-6-5 (paperback)

ISBN: 979-8-9996193-5-8 (digital)

CHAPTER 1

*M*iriam Troyer shifted on the hard wooden bench, adjusting her stiff apron as the preacher's voice echoed through her father's workshop. The scent of sawdust clung to the air, mingling with the faint burn of kerosene from the lanterns strung along the walls.

She usually loved this space: the neat rows of tools, the quiet hush of wood waiting to be shaped. But today the walls seemed to inch closer, the air thick with a pressure that made it hard to breathe. Three hours of church service in a room with no escape, no sky, and too many eyes.

She traced the edge of her *Ausbund*, her thumb skimming the familiar worn cover. Outside, frost curled along the windows, catching slivers of sunlight. If she squinted, she could make out the silhouettes of bare branches shifting in the wind. She slipped off her glasses and rubbed her eyes. The world refused to sharpen. Instead, a dull blur pooled in the center of her sight... a reminder of the thing no one dared speak aloud during fellowship.

But in the quiet hours of last night, they had.

She hadn't meant to listen. She'd gone downstairs for a glass of water, only to pause on the steps when she heard her parents' voices low in the kitchen. Not angry. Just tired. Worn and worried.

"She's the plainest of our *dochders*," her mother had whispered, each word landing like a stone. "The others were married long before they reached her age. And look at her: twenty-four next week, losing her sight, overweight, and not much to look at. Who would want to take on such a burden?"

Miriam had stood frozen, her hand gripping the stair rail. Her father's reply was calm but firm. "That's enough, Evelyn. She's the kindest of our *kinner*. She helps you every day and never complains. You speak like this is her fault, when you know it's the same disease my mother had. *Stargardt's*, the doctor called it. And *Mamm* lived a full life."

"She was diagnosed much later in life, and she had plenty of help." An edge returned to Evelyn's voice. "A young *fraa* needs to cook, read recipes, and keep a household. What kind of mother will she be if she can't read to her *kinner*?"

Miriam had blinked hard, her throat tight.

"She's not much for cooking now," she had added. "She's always outside in the woods. What sort of future is that?"

Their voices faded as she tiptoed back to her room and slid under her quilt. But the words had followed her there. They tangled in her thoughts, winding through her dreams.

Her mother's words still rang in her ears as the

preacher spoke on. About surrender. About trusting *Gott's* path. About endurance in a trial. She closed her eyes for a moment, feeling the slight pressure behind her lids. Not from pain, exactly, but from knowing what lay ahead.

She didn't mind the diagnosis… not in the way her mother did. She'd already come to terms with it. Mostly. What cut deeper was the way her mother saw her. As broken. As someone less-than. As someone to be managed, not trusted.

A nudge against her side startled her. "Number 720," her cousin whispered, tapping the hymnal in Miriam's lap.

Miriam straightened, humming the words softly. The song filled the space, voices gentle and reverent. But her mind wandered forward, toward three o'clock, when she'd meet Hannah, her best friend, for their walk in the woods.

With her boots crunching the snow, and the cold air brushing her cheeks, the quiet place between the trees was where she could think, breathe, and feel like herself again.

She pictured it clearly: the narrow trail behind the barns, the tall trees arching overhead, the creek that would be half-frozen but still singing its soft winter song. The hush of the woods always calmed her, soothed the loudest parts of her mind.

She wasn't afraid of going blind. Not really.

What terrified her more was the pity evident in her mother's eyes even before her vision failed completely.

That was the deeper loss. The one that didn't come with a diagnosis or a timeline. Just the slow erosion of confidence, of dignity. The silent way someone else's fear could strip your sense of who you were.

She would not let that happen. She hummed the next verse with quiet conviction.

Her fingers tapped the side of her hymnal in rhythm

with the song, steadying herself with the sound of the *g'mays'* voices rising and falling together. The deep baritone of her father's voice across the room. The faint, sweet tone of her cousin's song beside her. A dozen voices, blending, weaving something holy.

She turned her face back to the frost-glazed window.

The sunlight had shifted. It struck the glass in a different way now, brighter, almost dazzling. A thin line of gold shimmered across the ice crystals. Beyond it, the trees swayed as if stirred by something more than just wind.

A whisper, perhaps. A nudge.

The kind that stirred her heart when she stood still long enough to notice.

A reminder.

That the world hadn't gone dark yet, that even when it did, there would still be light in other places.

In the rustle of trees. In the promise of love. In the strength of her own voice, rising with the hymn. And she wasn't about to give up walking through that world. Not today. Not ever. No matter what her mother thought.

As Miriam helped clean up after church lunch, she glanced at the calendar on the kitchen wall. The date jumped out at her, *January 15th*. In all the recent eye doctor appointments and tests, she had practically forgotten her birthday was less than four days away. *Nee...* she wouldn't succumb to her mother's predictions. She would prove her wrong. She wouldn't let a diagnosis of *Stargardt disease* define her or limit what she could do.

As the last family pulled from the driveway, Miriam dried her hands and hurried upstairs. She pulled on a warmer sweater and leggings beneath her dress, eager to meet Hannah at their predetermined meeting spot. Nothing, not even her mother's doubts, could keep her from the one person who always saw her for who she truly was.

❧

OUTSIDE, a light dusting of snow covered the frozen ground, making for a perfect hike through the woods that stretched between Miriam's and Hannah's Northwestern Pennsylvania family farms. The air was crisp, and her breath curled in wispy tendrils as she made her way toward the trail that weaved throughout Willow Springs.

Before heading out, Miriam stopped at the row of white calf hutches lined up near the barn. Her father purchased young Holstein and Jersey calves every few months from the livestock auction, raising them until they were ready to be sold to Amish dairy farmers around the county.

Miriam's condition had prevented her from taking a regular job outside the home like most of her friends, so she had taken over the sole responsibility of feeding and caring for the calves. This allowed her father to focus on filling his custom-made furniture orders.

If she was honest with herself, there were days when she envied Hannah for being able to work at the Apple Blossom Inn, meeting new people and experiencing life beyond the farm.

But on the days when she saw real progress in a sick calf or when a weak one at last stood steady on its legs or eagerly drank its milk, she knew she wouldn't want to do anything else.

She leaned over the enclosure of the smallest calf, a brown-and-white Jersey that had struggled to gain weight since its arrival. It lifted its head at her approach, its soft muzzle pressing against her palm as it suckled on her bare finger. The odor of powdered calf milk clung to her woolen barn coat, a familiar and comforting smell.

"*Ach*, you'll be big and strong soon enough," she murmured, giving the calf's head a gentle pat before securing the enclosure.

Satisfied that all was well, she pulled her coat tighter around her and moved toward the King farm. The cold air stung her lungs, but she hardly noticed as she picked up her pace, eager to visit Hannah.

The snow-covered path stretched out before Miriam, draped in the hush of winter. The towering hardwoods, maples, and oaks stood bare, their skeletal branches dusted with snow, while clusters of pine trees kept their dark green needles, offering pockets of color amid the frosty landscape. The snow underfoot crunched softly as she made her way down the narrow path that led to Hannah.

A sudden rustling to her right sent a flurry of movement through the underbrush. Miriam stopped as a startled deer bounded across her path, its white tail flicking as it disappeared deeper into the woods.

Miriam sighed happily, taking in the peaceful stillness that followed. She breathed in the crisp, pine-scented air. For all the uncertainty in her life, this place—these woods —stood steady, unchanging. A quiet refuge she could always trust.

As she neared the edge of the forest, the land sloped downward toward the King farm. The big, century-old barn loomed ahead, its white paint faded from decades of use but still standing strong. Just as Miriam rounded the corner, the low rumble of an engine sputtering to life made her stop short.

MJ. Marvin J. King was one of many Marvins in the

King family, though Miriam had long since given up trying to sort them all out. Unlike his older *bruders*, MJ hadn't yet committed to baptism, still lingering in the freedom of *rumspringa* longer than most. Not that Miriam judged him for it… at least, she tried not to. It wasn't her place.

The beat-up old Ford truck grumbled as MJ backed it away from the barn. His father insisted he park it out of sight, not wanting a worldly vehicle sitting in plain view. Miriam watched as the truck inched backward, the tires slipping in the snow before they grabbed hold. Then, as if sensing her presence, MJ rolled down his window, grinning as he caught sight of her.

"Still stomping around in the woods, eh?" He raised his eyebrows and pushed his baseball cap up, a hat his father disapproved of just as much as the truck.

She crossed her arms and grinned. "And you're still stalling on making a decision, eh, MJ?"

His grin didn't falter. "*Ach*, no rush. *Gott* will catch me when He's ready."

Miriam huffed. "Or when you get tired of driving that old thing."

MJ laughed, the sound warm and easy. "I got something for you." He reached into the passenger seat and grabbed a small book, holding it out the window.

Miriam's heart lifted with surprise. This was their unspoken tradition, exchanging books whenever they crossed paths. She stepped forward and took it, flipping it over in her hands.

"Where'd you get this one?" she asked, scanning the title.

"I saw it at the second-hand store and thought of you," he answered with a shrug. "Figured you'd like it."

Miriam ran her gloved fingers over the worn cover, smiling despite herself. She might not always understand

MJ, but at least in this, they spoke the same language. She tilted her head, reading the title aloud with a curious cadence, "*Hiking the South Carolina Foothills Trail?*"

She had read many books before. Stories of family life, devotionals, and even the occasional forbidden sweet romance novel passed between friends. But this? This was different.

Without answering her question about why he thought she'd enjoy a book about hiking a trail over six hundred miles away, he simply grinned and tipped his cap. "Enjoy it." He shifted the truck into gear. "Let me know what you think."

The old Ford rumbled as he eased it back onto the snowy path, leaving Miriam with the book still in her hands. She tucked it into her coat pocket, shaking her head. She never knew what to make of Hannah's older and quite… unpredictable *bruder.*

Before she could think about it more, a burst of muddled colors caught her eye. Hannah's small frame and dark hair bounded beside her, her cheeks pink from the cold. "Finally," Hannah breathed, brushing a stray snowflake from her chin. "Ready?"

Miriam and Hannah had walked this section of the Spring Trail, which circled in and around Willow Springs more times than they could count. The five-mile stretch around their farms and along Willow Creek had become their sanctuary over the years, a place where words weren't always needed.

Normally, their walks were filled with a comfortable silence; the rhythm of their feet pounding the path spoke louder than words between them. But today was different.

Today, Miriam's thoughts weighed too heavily to keep inside.

For the first mile, she tried to ignore the lump forming in the back of her throat. She knew Hannah already understood; her mother had spoken to Hannah's mother just the day before. But still, the words burned inside her, waiting for release. She kicked a frozen clump of earth and took a deep breath.

"*Mamm* doesn't believe I have a future." The words came out quieter than she intended, but Hannah's head snapped toward her all the same.

"Not so?" Hannah replied, reaching out to stop Miriam's stride.

"*Jah*," Miriam replied, her voice stronger now. "I heard her say it. She thinks I'll be a burden, so much so that no man would ever want to marry me. That I won't be able to manage a family on my own." She swallowed hard, her breath misting in the cold air. "She thinks I'll never be anything more than what I am right now… just a girl on the brink of losing her sight."

Hannah forced Miriam to turn toward her. The compassion in her best friend's deep brown eyes made Miriam want to look away, but she held her gaze.

"Then prove her wrong, prove them all wrong. Your mother, the doctors, anyone who thinks your life is going to be limited by this. You're stronger than any of them know."

Miriam let out a small, shaky laugh. "You make it sound so simple."

"Because it is." Hannah reached for her gloved hand and squeezed it. "You have dreams, don't you? So chase them. Who says you have to live the way everyone expects you to?"

Miriam hesitated, then nodded. "I do have dreams.

And I've already promised myself I won't let anyone, not *Mamm*, not the doctors, not even my own fears, tell me what I can or can't do."

Hannah smiled, her cheeks rosy from the cold. "So, what's the first thing you're going to do to prove them all wrong?"

Miriam exhaled, glancing down the snowy path ahead of them. The trees seemed to stretch on forever, a reminder that the road forward wouldn't be easy. But for the first time in days, fear loosened its grip and something steadier rose in its place. Determination.

She turned to Hannah, her lips curving into a confident smile. "I guess I better start figuring that out."

Hannah grinned and tugged on Miriam's sleeve. "Then let's make it official."

A knowing look passed between them, and without another word, they veered off the trail toward a fallen hollow tree nestled deep in the woods. Years ago, they had buried a one-gallon glass jar with a metal lid inside a hollowed-out tree trunk, a secret time capsule of sorts. Over the years, they had added special trinkets, notes, and memories… things that only they knew about.

Hannah knelt in the snow and dug at the opening, her mittens brushing away the powder that had settled over the log. With ease, she pulled out the jar, its glass smudged with dirt but still intact. Inside, folded papers nestled alongside small tokens of their past.

Hannah ran her gloved fingers over the worn lid, her breath misting in the cold air as memories flickered through her mind. The first time they had buried something inside, they had been no more than ten years old. Two little girls, huddled in the woods, whispering their dreams into scraps of paper as if they were secrets too fragile to be spoken aloud.

Hannah had written her first note in the shaky penmanship of a child: "*I want to be a mother someday and have a house full of laughter*." She had drawn a tiny picture beside the words, a crude sketch of stick-figure children running through a field. Miriam had watched as she placed it inside, her young face filled with certainty.

Miriam's own dream had been different, more uncertain. "*I want to see the world,*" was all she had written, unsure even then what that truly meant. It had felt silly at the time; what did "seeing the world" mean for an Amish girl? And yet, she had written it anyway, tucking the paper inside as if, by some miracle, it might come true.

Now, years later, she pulled out the old notes, unfolding them carefully. Hannah's was still there, faded but clear. And so was hers. She traced the words with her fingertips, a strange lump forming, closing her throat. She had nearly forgotten this version of herself. The little girl who had dared to dream beyond the safety of her Amish community.

Hannah nudged her gently. "What are you thinking?"

Miriam swallowed, refolding the slip of paper. "That maybe I wasn't just being a foolish child when I wrote this."

A small smile played on Hannah's lips. "You weren't. And maybe it's time to write a new one."

Miriam hesitated, then took the pencil and paper Hannah pulled from her pocket. She stared at the blank page for a moment before writing, the words forming with surprising certainty:

"*I promise to live life fully, no matter what.*"

Hannah took the notepad and quickly scrawled beneath Miriam's words: "*I promise to remind you of this promise when you forget.*"

They signed their names and exchanged glances before

tucking the paper back inside the jar. With the lid sealed, Hannah placed it back in the hollow of the tree, covering the entrance with a small pile of snow and leaves.

Miriam dusted off her gloves and stood, feeling the slight whisper of the girl who had once dreamed of something more.

CHAPTER 2

*M*J shifted in his seat as the old Ford rumbled down the narrow, snow-packed lane leading away from the barn. The exhaust puffed out in thick white clouds, disappearing into the crisp January air. His father wouldn't be pleased that he'd lingered near the barn so long for all to see. But what did it matter? He wasn't baptized yet, which meant he had the freedom to come and go as he pleased... for now, at least.

He tightened his grip on the worn steering wheel and glanced out the rearview mirror. Miriam was still standing there, tucking the book he'd given her into her coat pocket.

A small smile tugged at the corner of his mouth before he shook his head and turned back to the road ahead. He wasn't sure why he had picked that book for her, at least, not at first.

But then, he had noticed things. The way her entire demeanor changed when she laced up her old hiking boots, how she moved through the woods with an ease he rarely saw in others. How she always carried that old, knotted branch as a walking stick, steady and sure. She didn't just walk; she belonged there, as if the woods were the one place she could truly breathe. And maybe, in that way, they weren't so different after all.

She just didn't know yet that he had followed the same path. That he had walked those same trails, taking in the quiet solitude just as she did. Maybe that's why he had chosen the book for her. Or maybe it was just an excuse. Either way, she was way out of his league... *always had been*. Too pretty, too kind, too... everything. Not that he was looking for anything serious. Not yet anyway.

MJ had never quite fit the mold of what an Amish man should be. He was shorter than all his *bruders*, and chubby for most of his youth, making him an easy target for teasing from older and stronger scholars. He had learned rapidly that he would never outmatch them physically, so he outpaced them in wit and knowledge instead. While they spent their time competing in volleyball and buggy races, he spent his hiding in the still corners of the barn with a book. Even now, he preferred the solitude of the written word, where the world made sense in a way that his own future did not.

The question of baptism loomed over him like a weight he wasn't sure he was ready to carry. It wasn't that he doubted his faith, but settling down meant giving up the dreams he had barely begun to explore.

His father had done it, his older *bruders* had done it, and in time, everyone expected that he would join the church too. But before that happened, he wanted to see something beyond these hills and barns. He wanted to know what lay beyond the same roads he had traveled his entire life.

And that's precisely what he was working toward. His job at the Feed & Seed was paying well enough, especially now that he could keep all his earnings instead of turning them over to his father. Every paycheck brought him one step closer to setting out and seeing the world... well, at least a small part of it. He wasn't looking for anything drastic, just enough to satisfy his curiosity before returning to the life he knew he'd eventually have to embrace.

That's why he had studied the Foothills Trail book for days before handing it to Miriam. It was a place where he could picture himself wandering through with nothing but his pack and the sound of his own footsteps.

He didn't know if the book would interest her the same way it had intrigued him, but he was eager to hear her thoughts. He'd never met another Amish person who loved books the way he did, but Miriam came close.

As the truck bounced over a rut in the road, he sighed and gave himself a mental shake. It was foolish to even entertain the thought of Miriam Troyer as anything more than a friend. She deserved someone better, someone taller, stronger, and definitely more settled. He was none of those things. A little too thick through the middle now, a little too plain, and nowhere near as charming as the other available young men in the community.

It would be easier to stay teetering on the fence between the Amish and *Englisch* worlds for as long as possible, avoiding his inevitable future if that was the path he'd choose. Perhaps when the time came to settle down, he could hope for someone as sweet as Miriam. But for now, he had plans to make, books to read, and a world waiting for him beyond the rolling hills of Pennsylvania.

His foot pressed the accelerator, and the truck roared toward town. The Feed & Seed was waiting, and so was the next customer that needed looking after. His time for adventure would come... just not yet.

~

WORK WAS SLOW THAT AFTERNOON, the lull between morning deliveries and late-day pickups stretching into a quiet, uneventful shift. MJ worked steadily, stacking fifty-pound bags of livestock feed onto pallets, his breath visible in the cool air of the warehouse. He was grateful for the rhythm of physical labor, the way it kept his mind from wandering too far into thoughts he didn't want to entertain.

The bell over the storeroom jingled, and when he glanced up, his stomach tightened. Bishop Schrock stepped inside, shaking the snow from his coat and stamping his boots. The bishop was a sturdy man, not unkind, but his presence always carried a weight of unspoken expectations.

"*Ach*, MJ." The bishop's voice was warm and friendly as he approached the counter. "Didn't expect to find you working today. Thought you might be home helping your *datt*."

MJ dusted his hands off on his trousers and stepped forward. "*Jah*, I work mornings on the farm, but I take shifts here to bring in extra money."

The bishop hummed in approval, nodding as he scanned the rows of stacked feed. "Hard work is good. It builds discipline. And extra earnings never hurt a young man preparing for a family of his own."

MJ forced a small smile, knowing where this conversation was headed.

The bishop leaned against the counter, folding his hands in front of him. "I've noticed you're taking your time with your decision."

MJ exhaled slowly. "Baptism?"

The bishop nodded. "*Jah*. We all have our own paths to

walk, but a man who lingers too long at the crossroads risks losing sight of the road altogether."

MJ swallowed hard, his fingers pressing into the rough wood of the counter.

The bishop's voice softened. "I know what it is to feel pulled in two directions. But we are not meant to wander. Our faith, our people, our way of life, it's a gift, even when it feels like a burden. Don't let the temptation of the unknown take you away from what *Gott* has already given you."

MJ nodded out of respect, but he had heard these words before from his father. But what if he wasn't chasing temptation? What if he was chasing clarity?

The bell jingled again, breaking the moment. An *Englisch* customer entered. A woman in her late fifties, dressed in a new Carhartt jacket, her auburn hair streaked with gray. She pulled her gloves off and smiled as she approached the counter.

"Afternoon," she greeted, setting a small shopping list on the counter. "I'm looking for some organic chicken feed. I just bought a little homestead outside of town, and I'm trying my hand at raising hens."

MJ nodded, already moving toward the back wall where the specialty feed was stored. "We've got a few options. First time keeping chickens?"

She laughed. "Oh, definitely. City girl turned hobby farmer. I have no idea what I'm doing, but I'm loving every second of it."

MJ hoisted a bag of feed onto the counter and rang up the total. "That'll get you started, at least."

She handed over payment, then glanced around the feed store. "I imagine you grew up doing farm work and raising livestock. It must be nice, knowing exactly what you're doing from one day to the next."

MJ hesitated, feeling Bishop Shrock's presence still nearby. "*Jah*," he muttered, hoping the bishop didn't notice his hesitation.

The woman smiled, nodding. "I admire that. I think there's something really special about people who stick to tradition. But there's something freeing about choosing your own path, too." She laughed, tucking her receipt into her pocket. "Not that I know what I'm doing half the time, but there's a thrill in figuring it out as you go."

MJ studied her for a moment, an unexpected twinge of longing rising in his chest as he pondered her parting words. "*Figuring it out as you go.*"

As she left, Bishop Shrock turned back to him. "It's natural to wonder, *sohn*. But don't do it so long that you lose your way back."

With that, he collected his order and walked out, leaving MJ standing at the counter, staring out at the world beyond the large window behind the counter, wondering what it would feel like to walk into it without knowing where he was going.

THE FARMHOUSE WAS QUIET; the only sound was the soft whisper of wind against the frosted windowpane. Wrapped in her quilt, Miriam nestled deeper into her bed, the bright glow of her headlamp shining a narrow beam over the worn pages of the book MJ had given her. She pulled the fabric of her quilt higher under her chin, the warmth comforting as she flipped the first few pages.

She had read plenty of books before, but this book was different. It wasn't about recipes, homemaking, or child-rearing, the books that lined the shelves of every Amish home she'd ever visited. It wasn't about how to be a good wife or an obedient daughter. But a book full of ways to challenge yourself and how to experience a part of the country few would ever see.

Her fingers tightened around the pages, her breath catching as she read about trails that stretched beyond Pennsylvania, paths carved into forests, winding over rivers, climbing toward ridgelines where the entire world could be seen from above. She had always loved walking, had always found peace in the woods behind the farm, but she had never considered that walking could be more than just a way to pass the time. That it could be a way to go somewhere.

Excitement curled in her stomach, but just as quickly, a small voice whispered back: "What would *Mamm* say if she knew you were reading such a book?"

Her mother made it known that she thought she spent too much time roaming the woods, insisting she was too old to be running wild and climbing trees like some stray animal. A proper Amish woman belonged in the kitchen, not gallivanting through the wilderness. And yet, she kept reading.

She read about the supplies a person would need: sturdy boots, a well-packed backpack, maps, and a compass to guide the way. She read about campfires glowing beneath a sky full of stars, of trails that stretched for miles, leading to places she had never even heard of before. It was a world entirely foreign to her, and yet, it called to something deep inside... a whisper of adventure.

Could she ever do something like this? Was it foolish to even dream about it? She hesitated before closing the book, tucking it under her pillow as if it were something secret. Something forbidden.

As she turned off her flashlight, she exhaled lightly,

staring at the ceiling. *Mamm* would never allow it for sure and certain. But still... the idea lingered.

THE MORNING STARTED OFF WRONG, whether from the lack of sleep or her mother hollering up the stairs, Miriam wasn't sure. The sky was scarcely streaked with light when a loud pounding on the stairs from her mother's broom handle made her jerk awake.

"Miriam!" Her mother's voice was heavy with urgency. "One of the calves didn't make it through the night. Your *datt* needs you to disinfect the shelter first thing."

Miriam groaned and pushed herself up, rubbing her tired eyes. She had hardly gotten any rest; her mind was still tangled with the thoughts from the night before. But there was no time to dwell on it now.

As soon as she stepped into the kitchen, her mother was already on her, her sharp tone cutting through the hazy morning air. "Hurry with your chores this morning. You need to get back inside and learn how to make a proper loaf of bread. It's high time you took an interest in something useful."

Miriam pulled on her boots, frustration bubbling to the surface. "I don't need to know how to bake. There's a grocery store just down the road. My family won't starve; I'm sure of it."

The words were out before she could stop them, and they hung in the air like burnt toast. She knew she had gone too far. Her mother's lips pressed together, her disapproval as thick as the aroma of fried bacon lingering in the air. But instead of waiting for a reply, Miriam turned on her heel and headed outside.

She had just stepped off the porch when the familiar

sound of MJ's truck broke the morning silence. He honked twice as he drove past, his grin wide as he waved through the closed window. Miriam shook her head, unable to hold back a small smirk. Before she could take another step, the front door slammed behind her. Her mother stepped onto the porch, crossing her arms against the morning chill. "That King boy is wasting his life," she muttered, her voice filled with condemnation. "I don't understand why Marvin M. doesn't do something about that obnoxious truck and that boy's wild ways."

Miriam hid a smile, pleased that MJ had managed to get under her mother's skin. She silently sent up an apology to the Lord for being so short with her mother, though she couldn't help but feel a small bit of satisfaction at the distraction MJ had caused.

As Miriam stepped off the porch, she couldn't understand why her mother wasn't more like Hannah's mother: kind, gentle, encouraging. A lump formed in her throat, and she shoved the thought away.

And again, she sent up another prayer, this time asking for forgiveness for her ungratefulness. The Lord had placed her in this family for a reason, even if she didn't always understand it.

As she moved toward the barn, her mother's voice trailed after her, barking instructions she already knew by heart. Miriam bit her lip, trying hard to honor her mother, not only in her words but in her actions as well.

THE WHIFF of hay and warm milk filled the barn as Miriam stepped inside, her boots clunking against the dirt floor. Her father stood near the barn sink, already hard at work. He had mixed up the milk and was slowly pouring it into a row of bottles, his hands steady from years of tending to the animals.

He looked up as she approached and gave her a small, knowing smile. "I'm sorry about the little Jersey. I know how much you tried to save her."

Miriam swallowed hard, nodding as she reached for one of the bottles. "I just thought maybe this time…"

Her father sighed, capping the last bottle. "Sometimes, these things are out of our control. I'll do my best to bring home some stronger ones today."

She wiped at her tired eyes, and her father's gaze sharpened.

"Did you remember to put in those drops the doctor gave you?"

She hesitated. "I was in a hurry to get outside. I'll do it once I go back in."

His brow furrowed, but he didn't push further. Instead, he handed her a bottle. "Be gentle on your mother. She only wants to make sure you have everything you need to face the world. It would make her happy to know she's shown you the things she taught your *schwesters.*"

Miriam pursed her lips but didn't argue. She knew he meant well, but the expectation weighed on her. As she loaded the filled bottles into the crate at her feet, she hesitated before speaking again. "*Datt*, did you ever have any dreams?

Her father stilled, his hands resting on the sink. A thoughtful silence filled the space before he spoke. "I wanted to learn how to fly a plane."

Miriam's eyes widened. "Really?"

He chuckled. "*Jah*. Not exactly practical for an Amish man, is it? But it has always fascinated me. The way they lift off, how something so heavy can soar through the sky." He sighed, his gaze drifting to the open barn doors. "I suppose it wasn't what *Gott* had planned for me. But still, whenever I hear one overhead, I stop whatever I'm doing just to listen and to watch. Something about the sound of the engine, the wings stretching wide, still makes me wonder."

Miriam studied him, her thoughts swirling. "So... sometimes dreams just stay dreams?"

He nodded slowly. "Sometimes, *jah*. And sometimes, they shape the way we see the world, even if we never live them out."

Miriam picked up the crate and headed back outside. She thought again about the book under her pillow, the trail she had read about, and the way something inside her had stirred at the idea of it. Maybe her father was right. Maybe some dreams weren't meant to be chased. But then something whispered inside her head, and she wasn't ready to give up just yet.

She wondered out loud, "Aren't dreams meant to be followed?"

Miriam's chores were finished; the calves fed and their enclosures cleaned. But she wasn't quite ready to head back inside just yet. She moved back to the barn and stood just inside the open barn door, leaning against the wooden frame as she pulled off her work gloves and flexed her fingers against the morning chill. The scent of hay and powdered milk clung to her coat, mixing with the crisp winter air.

Her gaze drifted to the small woodworking shop across the yard, where a steady swirl of smoke curled from the chimney, rising and twisting against the pale blue sky. Her father was already hard at work, the rhythmic hum of the planer shaving layers off rough wood echoing from within the metal building.

She closed her eyes for a moment, listening. Sounds had begun to take on a sharper clarity lately, filling in the spaces where her eyesight was beginning to wane. The soft rasp of the blade against the wood, the distant caw of a crow perched high in the trees, even the wind shifting through the bare branches, all of it seemed more pronounced, more vivid than before.

When she opened her eyes again, she fixed her gaze on the swirling smoke, trying to commit the image to memory. She wanted to remember it, to hold on to it in case there ever came a day when she could no longer make out the delicate wisps against the sky.

Or maybe, she admitted to herself, she was stalling.

Her boots scuffed against the barn floor as she shifted her weight. She knew what waited for her inside. Her mother was ready with a sharp word and a lesson in baking that Miriam had no interest in learning. She could think of a dozen things she'd rather do than spend the morning measuring flour and kneading dough. Among them was finding an excuse to go into town, to step into the quiet sanctuary of the library and lose herself in another book about hiking adventures.

The idea of it tugged at her, tempting her with the thought of new stories, of trails and places far beyond this small patch of farmland. But she knew better than to entertain that thought for long. Her mother expected her inside, and there was no getting around it.

Miriam sighed, pulling her coat tighter and taking a moment to straighten up the barn, brushing stray bits of straw from the walkway and ensuring everything was in its place. Then, she squared her shoulders and started toward the *haus*.

She would face whatever the morning held, even if it was just another reminder of all the ways she and her mother would never quite see eye to eye.

Miriam stepped into the too-warm kitchen, the aroma of yeast and flour already thick in the air. The farmhouse oven crackled as the fire within glowed hot, and her mother was already at the counter, her hands working the dough with practiced precision. Despite the cozy scent and steady warmth, something in her mother's rigid stance turned the air cold.

Miriam moved to the basin to wash her hands, her mother's sharp eyes tracking her every motion. "Took you long enough," she muttered, kneading the dough with force. "If you don't learn now, what will you do when you have a family of your own to feed? If that ever happens."

Miriam paused, her fingers gripping the worn dish towel a little too tightly. "Why do you always speak like that?"

Her mother sighed heavily, slapping the dough onto the floured surface. "Like what?"

"Like my future has already been decided for me." Miriam turned, drying her hands as she studied her mother. "You make it sound as if my life is over before it has even begun."

Her mother shook her head. "I'm only being practical. You act as if life is a storybook, as if everything will work itself out because you want it to. But that's not how the world works. One day, your father and I will be too old to take care of ourselves. Who will care for us if you cannot even bake a loaf of bread?"

The words cut deeper than Miriam wanted to admit.

She set the towel aside and moved to the counter, pressing her hands into the warm mound of dough. "So that's what you think? That I'll never be capable of taking care of anyone?"

Her mother's hands stilled, and for a brief moment, silence filled the kitchen. Then, with a tired sigh, she shook her head. "You're different from the other girls. You always have been. Your *schwesters* never questioned the way things were. They learned their duties, married good men, and settled into life as they should."

Miriam's jaw tightened. "And because I don't fit that mold, you think I'll never have a family? Never be able to manage myself?"

Her mother didn't answer right away. Instead, she focused on shaping the dough with skill that only came from years of practice, her fingers working methodically. "I think you live with your head in the clouds. Always out wandering, always dreaming of things that don't matter. The world is not as kind as you believe it to be. You'd do better to accept what is, rather than chase after what will never be."

Miriam inhaled deeply, pressing her frustration into the dough beneath her hands. She respected her mother, but she would not accept these words over her life. "I don't believe *Gott* gave me this life just to watch it pass me by. I won't settle for less than what I know I am capable of."

Her mother let out a small scoff. "And what exactly do you think you're capable of?"

Miriam lifted her chin, meeting her mother's gaze without hesitation. "More than you think."

A hint of something… worry, maybe even regret, crossed her mother's aging features, but it was gone just as quickly. With a sigh, she returned to the bread, kneading with renewed force. "Finish with that. The oven won't wait forever," she snapped.

Miriam nodded, forcing her frustration into the steady rhythm of her hands working the dough. She wasn't looking for approval. She had long since given up on that, but she refused to let her mother's doubts become her own. Her future was hers to shape, no matter who failed to see it.

CHAPTER 3

*T*he tension in the King's household was thick enough to cut with a knife. The dinner table was set with steaming bowls of potato soup, but MJ barely tasted a bite. Across from him, his father sat rigid, his spoon scraping against his bowl in slow, deliberate motions. MJ ate silently, his eyes darting between his parents as if waiting for the inevitable storm to break.

It came sooner than he expected.

"I got an earful from Evelyn Troyer this afternoon," their father, Marvin M., said, as he set his spoon down with a dull clink against the table. His gaze leveled at MJ. "Says your truck is an eyesore, but worse than that, it's a noise nuisance. Says you come and go at all hours, and the noise rattles her kitchen windows."

MJ's grip on his spoon tightened. He'd learned the hard way that backtalk would do no good, though his jaw twitched when backed in a corner.

MJ's appetite vanished. He pushed his bowl away slightly and tensed at his father's words. He had known this conversation was coming, but that didn't make it any easier, as he swallowed his words instead of voicing them.

"It's time to choose. Us or that truck," his father snarled.

MJ's shoulders stiffened. His father had never been one to mince words, but this sounded final, like a closing door he wasn't ready to step through. Across the table, Hannah shifted uncomfortably, but she remained silent.

His father studied him for a long moment. "Move that truck out of sight and far away from the house and barn."

MJ gave a curt nod in return and excused himself from the table. Hannah watched him carefully as he grabbed his coat and headed for the barn. His steps were brisk, but not from eagerness... more like the restless energy of a man walking off frustration.

THE COLD AIR circled MJ's head as he puffed out long sighs. The barn, once a place of purpose, now closed in around him, each chore another shackle keeping him tied to a future he didn't want. He reached for a grain scoop, gripping the handle tightly as he forced himself to focus. But all he could think about was the woodchuck trap he had set near the south field last week, how the animal had fought against the bars, clawing at the edges, desperate for an escape. He knew how that felt. And lately, every time he stepped into this barn and ran his hands over the rough wood of the stalls, he felt more and more like the animal in that trap. Hannah's footsteps crunched in the snow behind him, but he didn't turn. He already knew why she was here.

"You alright?" Hannah's voice was soft but knowing.

MJ exhaled sharply, not turning right away as he

grabbed a bucket and started filling it with grain. "What do you think?"

Hannah leaned against the post beside him, pulling her coat tighter around her. "I think you're about ready to explode."

MJ gave a humorless chuckle. "*Jah*, well, wouldn't be the first time."

She didn't say anything immediately but then asked, "You're not thinking about leaving… *are you?*"

MJ paused, his hand tightening around the handle of the bucket. He glanced at her, his eyes dark in the dim barn light.

"I don't know. Maybe. What else am I supposed to do? *Datt* keeps pushing me to make a decision I'm not ready to make."

Hannah sighed, kicking a loose bit of hay with the toe of her boot. "I don't know. But running off won't make it easier."

MJ smirked, shaking his head. "Maybe not. But it sure sounds nice right about now."

Hannah whispered, "Just don't do anything too reckless… *please.*"

MJ met her eyes and lifted his chin. "I'll try." But as she turned to head back inside, he was almost certain he couldn't keep that promise.

HANNAH HESITATED at the border of the darkened path, her breath curling in the cold air as she pulled her wool coat tighter around her shoulders. The trail between the King and Troyer farms was familiar, but tonight, something had shifted. Each step pressed deeper into the earth, as if her thoughts had gathered weight and followed her like a shadow.

She had no intention of going back inside after dinner, not after seeing the way her father's words had set MJ's jaw like stone. He was pushing too hard, trying to mold MJ into something he wasn't, just like Miriam's mother was doing to her. And Hannah was terrified that if something didn't change soon, they would both slip away from her forever.

By the time she reached the Troyer farmhouse, her fingers were numb from the cold. She knocked firmly on the door, shifting from one foot to the other as she waited. A moment later, Miriam appeared, her expression shifting from surprise to concern.

"Hannah? What are you doing out here so late?"

"I need to talk to you. Can I come in?"

"Of course." Miriam didn't hesitate and stepped aside, letting the warmth of the house welcome her in.

Miriam led Hannah past her mother, who sat stone-faced, working on a needlepoint project, scarcely acknowledging the girls as they headed up the stairs.

THE SCENT of fresh bread still lingered in the air, a reminder of the very thing Miriam had been forced to spend her day doing. The more batches they baked, the more relentless her mother had gotten. She'd corrected her every movement, every attempt at kneading, and every misplaced measurement. Miriam had tried to keep her frustration at bay, but the way her mother had hovered over her had been suffocating.

Now, as Miriam led Hannah to her room, she couldn't shake the feeling that her mother's words were still clinging to her like a too-tight dress. "*You have to learn to be useful, Miriam. You can't just run wild through the woods forever. What help will you be if you can't keep a home?*"

The words echoed in her mind, much like her mother's constant disapproving glances throughout the day. Miriam knew her mother wanted what she thought was best for her, but what if her version of *best* wasn't meant for Miriam at all?

Once inside the bedroom, Miriam shut the door and turned to Hannah. "Alright, what's wrong?"

Hannah let out a heavy sigh, sinking onto the end of Miriam's bed. "It's MJ. *Datt* is pushing him harder than ever. MJ hardly said a word at dinner, and that's what scares me. When he doesn't argue, it means he's already made up his mind about something. And I think he's planning to leave. For good."

Miriam's stomach twisted. "Leave?" she repeated, stunned. "You mean leave *leave*?"

Hannah nodded, her expression tight with worry. "I don't think he wants to just run off for a few nights like the other boys do during *rumspringa*. I think he's really considering leaving the Amish altogether. And I don't know how to stop him."

Miriam sat down beside her, her thoughts spinning. "What can I do?"

Hannah turned to her, eyes pleading. "He'll listen to you. Maybe if he had a reason to stay, he wouldn't go."

Miriam's brow furrowed. "Hannah..." She hesitated. "Are you asking me to—?"

"I just mean... maybe if he had something, *someone*, to make staying here worthwhile, he'd change his mind." Hannah's words rushed out.

A prick of unease settled on Miriam. She knew what Hannah was asking. What she wasn't saying outright, but it pressed against her like a heavy quilt, suffocating. "You're not asking me to pretend to be interested in him just to make him stay, are you?"

Hannah didn't answer right away, and that silence was enough. She hadn't meant to ask that, not consciously, but deep down, yes, that was exactly what she was hoping for.

Miriam's stomach twisted. She stood abruptly, needing space, needing air. "Hannah, that's not right. I can't trick him into staying. That's not fair to him, or to me."

Hannah stood too, reaching for Miriam's hand, her expression pleading. "I'm not asking you to trick him. Just… talk to him. Be his friend. Maybe if he realizes he's not alone in feeling like this, he'll reconsider."

Miriam swallowed hard, her pulse fluttering with uncertainty. She hated this feeling, this tug-of-war between what she knew was right and what she feared losing. What if she did talk to MJ? What if she planted a seed in his mind that kept him tethered to a life he didn't truly want? Would that be any better than her own mother forcing her into a mold she didn't fit?

But then again, what if Hannah was right? What if all he needed was someone to remind him that he wasn't alone? That staying didn't have to mean surrendering.

Her thoughts spun in endless circles, crashing against each other with no clear answer. She'd never been one to manipulate, to sway someone's path with careful words. And yet, the thought of MJ leaving, of never seeing him again, never exchanging another book, never sharing another quiet moment of understanding, sent a pang through her that she couldn't ignore.

She hesitated, then sighed quietly. "I'll talk to him. But I won't lie. I won't make him believe something that isn't true."

And she prayed, deep in her heart, that she wasn't

leading him, or herself, into something neither of them could undo.

Hannah's face lit up with relief. "That's all I ask."

Miriam hesitated, then took a deep breath. "If I do this, if I try to talk to him, I need you to promise me something too."

Hannah frowned. "What is it?"

Miriam looked away for a moment before meeting her friend's eyes. "Don't tell MJ or anyone about my eyesight. I don't want anyone to know. Not yet."

Hannah's expression softened. "Why?"

"Promise me, Hannah. If I do this, I need to know that part of my life is still mine to share when I'm ready."

Hannah nodded without hesitation. "I promise."

Miriam released the breath she hadn't realized she was holding. "Alright then. I'll do what I can, but I'm not making any promises."

THE KITCHEN WAS warm and filled with the traces of frying eggs and toast, but the tension at the breakfast table was as thick as the steam rising from the coffee pot. Miriam sat quietly, her hands folded in her lap as she waited for the right moment to speak. She had already been outside in the biting cold, tending to the calves and finishing her morning barn chores, and now, as she sat at the table, she tried to muster the courage to ask for something she already knew her mother would disapprove of.

She took a slow breath, glancing between her parents. "I was wondering if I could hire a driver to take me to the library today."

Her mother's fork stopped midway to her mouth. She lowered it with a sharp clink against her plate, her lips tightened in disapproval. "The library?" she repeated, as if Miriam had just asked for something completely unreasonable. "And what do you need more books for?"

Miriam shifted in her seat. "A winter storm is coming, and I'd like to have something new to read while we're stuck inside."

Her mother sneered as she tore off a piece of toast and mopped up the runny egg yolk off her plate. "Reading, always reading. Maybe if you spent half as much time learning to darn socks or cutting out a new shirt for your *datt* as you do burying your nose in those books, you'd be prepared for real life."

Miriam swallowed back her frustration. "*Mamm*, I do my fair share around here. I just—"

"You just want to waste time on things that won't serve you in the long run," her mother interrupted, spreading jam onto her toast with a firm swipe of the knife. "You should be using your free time to prepare for the life you'll have, not getting lost in stories."

A heavy silence settled over the table until her father set his coffee cup down and spoke, his voice calm but firm. "Evelyn, let the girl read. We don't know how long her eyes will allow for such luxuries. If books bring her joy, then I say she should have them."

Miriam glanced up at her father, warmth spreading through her chest at his words. He was a quiet man, but when he spoke, his words carried weight.

Her mother said nothing more, though the disapproval in her eyes was unmistakable.

Her father turned back to Miriam, reaching for another sausage patty. "If you're going to town, you might as well be useful. I've got a few things I need from the hardware store. I'll write out a list."

Miriam nodded swiftly, eager to take the permission while she had it. "*Denki*, I'll call the driver after breakfast."

Her mother huffed but didn't argue further. Miriam could feel her disapproval radiating across the table, but she refused to let it dampen her spirit. The library called to her, and for once, she had permission to answer.

THE MORNING AIR WAS CRISP, and the scent of hay and livestock was thick as MJ stepped into the barn. His father was already there, mucking out stalls. The rhythmic sounds of the farm waking up filled the space: the lowing of cattle, the clatter of metal stanchions, and the distant crow of a rooster greeting the dawn.

MJ had just reached for a pitchfork when his father's voice cut through the early morning stillness.

"You need to start thinking about the future."

MJ exhaled sharply, gripping the wooden handle tighter. "Didn't we just talk about this last night?"

His father ignored his protest. "I mean it. You're the last one left. This farm is going to be yours one day, and it's time you started acting like it."

MJ clenched his jaw, shoving the pitchfork into the hay pile with more force than necessary. "I do my share. I work the farm, I have a job at the Feed & Seed. What more do you want from me?"

His father stepped closer, his tone unrelenting. "I want you to take responsibility. Your *bruders* have moved on, they have families of their own, but this farm needs someone to keep it running. That someone is you. And not just the farm… your mother and I will need looking after one day. That's how it works. You'll take over the big *haus*, and we'll move into the *doddi haus*. You'll be responsible for keeping this place going, making sure it thrives for your own family someday. That's the way it's always been."

MJ's chest tightened. The words suffocating. His future had been decided for him long before he had a say in it. His *bruders* had their freedom, their own lives. And him? He was expected to stay behind, to carry the burden of tradition like a yoke around his neck.

"I never said I wanted that," he muttered.

His father's expression hardened. "It's not about what you want. It's about what's right. This is your duty, to this farm, to your family. Your *mamm* and I aren't getting any younger. Someday soon, it'll all fall to you."

MJ swallowed hard, his frustration bubbling dangerously close to the surface. "And what if I don't want it? What if I don't want to spend my life milking cows and fixing fences? What if I want to see what else is out there?"

His father's eyes darkened, disappointment etched into every line on his face. "You sound just like one of them *Englischers*," he muttered. "Selfish. Always chasing after things that don't matter instead of standing firm in what does. The Lord gave us this life for a reason. You don't just walk away from it because you think there's something better."

MJ's entire body tensed up with frustration. He wanted to argue, wanted to tell his father that he wasn't being selfish, he just wanted a choice. But he knew it wouldn't matter. His father had already made up his mind about what his life should be.

Instead of replying, he turned on his heel and made his way toward the back corner of the barn, where the light barely reached. Out of sight, he reached into his coat pocket and pulled out his bank book, flipping it open with cold, stiff fingers. The numbers stared back at him, and he quickly ran through the calculations in his head. It wasn't enough… not yet.

He let out a slow breath, his pulse steadying as he estimated how many more months of work at the Feed & Seed it would take. Five? Six? If he cut back on unnecessary spending, maybe less. Just a little longer, and then he could leave.

His father's voice snapped him back to the present. "MJ! Did you hear what I just said?"

MJ's entire body jumped. He wanted to argue. But what was the point? The pull of it pressed down on his chest like the heavy, frozen ground of the fields in winter. He needed more time. More months working at the Feed & Seed. More nights slipping away to stockpile what he could. His pulse pounded in his ears, the walls of the barn feeling smaller, tighter, like they were closing in.

He shoved the book back into his pocket and stalked toward the barn entrance, his boots kicking up loose hay as he went. "I'm late for work," he called over his shoulder. "We'll have to finish this conversation another day."

His father started to respond, but MJ didn't wait to hear it. He climbed into his truck, slammed the door shut, and turned the key in the ignition. The old engine rumbled to life, drowning out whatever his father was saying.

As he pulled out of the barnyard, he gripped the steering wheel, his knuckles whitening with the pressure. The walls of his world seemed to close in tighter with every mile. Just a few more months. Then he'd be free.

MIRIAM WANDERED through the quiet aisles of the library, running her fingers along the spines of the books as she searched for something, anything that could satisfy the growing curiosity she couldn't shake.

Her steps slowed as she reached the travel section, and she tilted her head, scanning the shelves for something that might hold the answers she was looking for.

And then she saw him.

MJ sat cross-legged on the floor, books scattered around him in a semi-circle. His head was bent, his fingers idly flipping through the pages of one of the books in his lap. Miriam took a step closer, her heart skipping a beat at the unexpected sight of him.

He looked up at the sound of her approach, surprise flashing in his eyes before he quickly straightened. "Miriam?" He glanced around as if caught doing something he shouldn't be. "Didn't expect to see you here."

She smiled. "Didn't expect to find you sitting on the floor, either."

He gave a sheepish chuckle, closing the book he'd been holding. "Lunch break. Thought I'd check out a couple of new books while I had the time."

Miriam glanced down at the titles scattered around him and lowered herself onto the floor beside him. "What are you looking at?"

He gestured toward the pile. "Just a few things." She read the spines: *The Best in Tent Camping, A Backpacker's Handbook,* and *Camping Etiquette.*

She raised an eyebrow. "Are you planning a trip sometime soon?"

He hesitated before shrugging. "Just dreaming." He offered her a lopsided grin. "Never hurts to dream a little, *jah*?"

Miriam nodded, tracing the spine of a book cover with her fingers. "That's actually why I'm here, too."

"Oh?"

She hesitated, feeling uncharacteristically shy. "I was hoping to find another book about hiking. I, um… I really enjoyed the one you gave me about the Foothills Trail."

His eyebrows arched. "You did?"

Miriam nodded. "I didn't even know there were trails like that … that people travel just to hike. It's fascinating to me."

MJ leaned back against the bookshelf, watching her. "So, what was it that you found interesting?"

She hesitated, gathering her thoughts before answering. "It's the thought of adventure, I think. I love walking in the woods around our farm, it's where I feel most at peace. But I never realized that people make a whole life out of hiking. That they go and see new places just by walking. It's… it's something I never thought about before."

For a moment, he didn't say anything, just studied her like he was seeing her in a new light. She swallowed, suddenly remembering Hannah's request. She cleared her throat, forcing herself to sound casual. "Maybe we could talk about it more sometime?"

She knew how bold that sounded, how unusual it was for a girl to suggest spending time alone with a man, even in friendship. But she wasn't suggesting anything improper, just conversation. "Just as friends, of course."

He smiled slightly. "Of course?"

Her cheeks warmed, but she held his gaze. He seemed to consider it for a moment before nodding. "If the storm doesn't snow us in, how about we meet at the Sandwich Shoppe Wednesday morning? Get a coffee, talk some more?"

Miriam's heart gave a small, unexpected jolt, but she kept her voice even. "That sounds nice."

MJ grinned. "And if the storm does snow us in, no

worries. My truck can go through anything. I could pick you up."

She shook her head, smiling despite herself. "We'll see about that."

MJ picked up the book about *Camping Etiquette* and handed it to her. "Here, you might like this one. It covers the basic things every camper should know."

Miriam took it, running her fingers over the cover before glancing at the book he picked up for himself—*A Backpacker's Handbook.*

"We can read them and discuss them on Wednesday," he suggested.

She liked that idea. "Sounds like a plan."

As she reached for a book from the shelf on hiking to beautiful waterfalls, her hand slowed, and her gaze dropped, suddenly unsure in his presence. Perhaps it was the idea of adventure or the realization that, for the first time in her life, she had met someone who yearned for more than the future their Amish traditions had mapped out for them. Someone who wouldn't settle for the exact twenty-five miles that defined their Amish community. Someone who, like her, wondered what else lay beyond the familiar roads they had always known.

CHAPTER 4

The morning after the storm, the Troyer farm was blanketed in a thick layer of snow, the kind that made buggies nearly impossible to maneuver. Miriam had spent the early hours shoveling a path to the barn, tending to the calves, and making sure the animals were fed, all while feeling the strain of what she was about to do pressing against her chest.

At breakfast, she waited for the right moment before setting her fork down and taking a deep breath. "I'm going into town this morning to get coffee with a friend."

Her mother scarcely glanced up from buttering her bread. "Who and how? You must realize the condition of the roads."

Miriam hesitated. "MJ King."

The room went completely silent.

"Absolutely not. You're a baptized member of the church, and it is highly improper for you to be riding anywhere with an unmarried man. Especially in his *Englisch* vehicle."

Miriam braced herself. "We're just friends. It's nothing improper."

Her mother let out a sharp breath. "Nothing improper? Miriam, do you realize how this looks? Riding in that boy's *truck*—" she practically spat the word. "Without supervision? You might as well announce to the entire community that you have no intention of honoring the *Ordnung*!"

Miriam's heart pounded, but she refused to back down. "The snow is too deep to take the buggy out, and I'm not walking six miles in it. MJ offered to take me into town, that's all."

"That's all?" Her mother spat. "This is how it starts. One little act of defiance turns into another. Next thing you know, you'll be running wild like those *Englisch* girls with no sense of decency. What would your *schwesters* think? What would the bishop think?"

Miriam clenched her jaw. "They would think that I'm an adult, perfectly capable of making my own choices."

Her mother let out an exasperated noise and turned to her father, looking for support. "Are you hearing this? Say something!"

Miriam glanced at her father, her pulse quickening. He had been silent this whole time, drinking his coffee, listening to the exchange with his usual calm demeanor. Now, he set his cup down, his gaze flicking between them.

For a long moment, he didn't say a word.

Then, to Miriam's surprise, a small smile tugged at the corner of his lips before he promptly covered it with another sip of coffee.

Evelyn gasped. "Bennie!"

He cleared his throat, his expression returning to its usual neutral state. "Evelyn, the girl has shoveled half the farm before breakfast. If she wants to go into town for a coffee, I don't see the harm."

Her mother looked utterly betrayed. "You can't possibly think this is acceptable."

He shrugged. "It's not like she's leaving the state."

The low rumble of MJ's truck carried through the crisp morning air as he pulled up, his tires crunching over the snow-packed drive. A knock at the door abruptly ended the argument.

Evelyn glared at her daughter, her eyes burning with warning. "If you walk out that door, you leave without my blessing."

Miriam's heart pounded so hard she could feel it in her throat. Her mother's sharp glare, the warning in her voice, it all pressed down on her like an iron weight. The good, obedient daughter inside her wanted to yield, to bow her head and murmur an apology. To back away from the door, from MJ, from the defiance simmering just beneath her ribs.

She had never outright challenged her mother before. Not like this. She had always taken the quieter route, choosing her battles, nodding along when it was easier than arguing. Pushing back meant conflict, and conflict with Evelyn Troyer was like standing in the middle of a storm, waiting for the winds to tear you apart.

She could still back out. She could sit back down at the table, let her mother's words settle like stones in her stomach, and go about her day as if she had never thought about leaving. It would be easier. It would be expected.

But then she thought of the way MJ had looked at her in the library, as if she wasn't just another girl meant to fall into the mold laid out for her. Like she was capable of more than the world she had always known.

And then she thought of herself, who she wanted to be,

not who everyone expected her to be. The words left her lips before she could stop them. "I'm sorry you feel that way, *Mamm*. But I'm going."

Her mother gasped as if struck. But before she could respond, before Miriam could let fear claw its way back into her chest, she grabbed her coat and stepped out the door, letting the cold air hit her like a baptism into something new.

MJ leaned against the porch railing, hands stuffed into his coat pockets. He raised a brow as she approached, clearly having overheard the tension inside. "Everything alright?"

Miriam forced a small smile, though her heart still pounded behind her ribcage. "Let's just say you may not be one of my mother's favorite people right now."

MJ grinned, opening the passenger door for her. "Wouldn't be the first time I got under her skin."

As she climbed in and shut the door, she glanced back toward the house. Through the window, she saw her father take another slow sip of coffee while her mother stood rigid with frustration, staring out the window. For a moment, she thought she saw her father's smile return, just the faintest, knowing curve of his lips.

Miriam turned away, her hands twisting in her lap as MJ pulled out of the driveway. The battle of wills between her and her mother had just begun. And for the first time, she had won this round.

THE SANDWICH SHOPPE was a familiar place, the kind of small-town café that always smelled of fresh yeast rolls, brewed coffee, and a hint of cinnamon from the sticky buns displayed behind the counter. It was a favorite meeting place for young Amish couples, a quiet corner of Willow Springs where conversation could flow easily, away from the watchful eyes of their families.

As MJ pulled the truck into a parking space, Miriam's stomach fluttered. She had no idea why. They were just meeting as friends. Just talking. And yet, something about it felt different. Maybe because she had never openly defied her mother before, or maybe because she had never sat down alone with a man in public like this. Or perhaps because she wasn't quite sure what MJ wanted out of this unofficial date, or what she wanted, for that matter.

She followed him inside, the bell over the door jingling softly as they entered. The warm scent of coffee filled the air, wrapping around her like a comforting embrace. A few other customers sat at tables, mostly young couples speaking in hushed voices.

Miriam chose a small table near the window, pulling her coat off and draping it over the chair. Outside, the snow-covered trees lined Main Street, their branches weighed down by the recent storm. A few cars passed slowly, their tires crunching against the packed snow, and a buggy trailed behind, the horse's breath visible in the cold morning air.

MJ tugged off his gloves and flexed his hands, rubbing them together for warmth. "I'll get the coffee," he offered.

She nodded, grateful for the moment to settle herself as he made his way to the counter. She folded her hands on the table, tracing the smooth wood with her fingertips as she tried to calm the lingering nerves. This was just coffee. Just conversation.

MJ returned a few minutes later, setting two steaming mugs on the table before sliding into the chair across from her, wrapping his hands around his cup. "What'd you think of *Camping Etiquette*?"

Miriam smiled easily, grateful for the easy topic. "It was... informative. I never knew there were so many rules for something as simple as camping. Pack out what you pack in, bury your waste, don't feed the wildlife, seems like a lot of effort just to sleep outside."

He chuckled. "That's what I thought at first too. But if you're going to do something, might as well do it right."

She took a sip of her coffee, savoring the warmth before glancing at him. "And *A Backpacker's Handbook*?"

He exhaled through his nose, shaking his head. "It just made me want to leave even more."

His voice had lost the lightness from a moment ago, and Miriam noticed the shift in his expression. The tension in his jaw, the way his fingers drummed against the ceramic mug like he was pondering sharing something important.

He stared into his coffee. "My *datt* expects me to take over the farm and big *haus* when he and *Mamm* retire, spend the rest of my life working the same land my grandfathers did."

He paused, took a long sip, and glared out the window before continuing. "But what if that's not what I want?

Miriam hesitated, staring down at her coffee. She had always sensed something restless about MJ, something simmering just beneath the surface, but she had never put much thought into why.

Now, hearing it from him directly, it clicked into place; he was just as trapped as she was. The cloak of expectation, of tradition, of a life chosen for them before they even had a say, bound them both in ways neither of them had spoken about before. But saying it out loud? That was something different entirely.

"I think that we're both expected to be something we're not."

MJ looked up at her, his eyes searching hers. "Your mother?"

She nodded. "She wants me to be like my *schwesters*, settled, content, happy in a home filled with children, baking bread and darning socks." She let out a soft sigh. "But that's never been me. I don't enjoy baking, and I have no desire to spend my days keeping house."

MJ's lips quirked up at the corner. "I've never understood why Amish women go through all that trouble. Baking bread when you can buy it for next to nothing at the store? Seems like a waste of time."

Miriam let out a laugh, surprised by his bluntness. "If my mother heard you say that, she'd have a fit."

He grinned. "Probably. But really, why make life harder than it has to be? Like standing out in the cold hanging clothes in the winter when there's a perfectly good laundromat with dryers in town? It makes no sense."

Miriam shook her head, still laughing. "You'd be run out of the community if anyone heard you say that."

"Maybe," he admitted, his grin lingering. "But you're laughing, so I'll count that as a win."

She met his gaze, warmth spreading in her chest at the easy way he made her smile. She had never seen this side of MJ before; his honesty made her feel at ease, like they were just two people sharing a simple moment. And she found herself liking it. Maybe more than she should.

MJ WRAPPED his hands around his coffee mug, watching Miriam as she gazed out the window, her fingers absently tracing the rim of her cup. Something about the way she looked at the world made him curious. She wasn't like the other Amish girls he knew; content with their future, eager to step into the roles laid out for them. But Miriam was unsettled, almost like she was searching for something more.

"What do you see in your future?" he asked, his voice casual but laced with genuine curiosity.

Her reaction was immediate. She flinched, just slightly, but enough for him to notice. Her shoulders tensed, and for the briefest moment, her gaze flickered downward before she forced a small smile.

MJ narrowed his eyes. He hadn't missed it. "What? What did I say?"

"Nothing," she shook her head, but there was something off in the way she said it. A little too forced, a little too careful.

MJ studied her, tempted to push, but something told him not to. He knew the look of someone guarding a secret, someone not ready to let it all out just yet. He wasn't sure why, but instinct told him that whatever had caused her to react like that wasn't something small.

She shook her head, looking down at her coffee. "I just... I don't fit the typical Amish woman mold, and that grates on my mother's nerves. She's spent years trying to shape me into someone I'm not."

She let out a breath, pushing a stray piece of hair behind her ear. "I hate challenging her. I hate going against her. It feels wrong, like I'm disappointing her. But at the same time, I've spent my whole life taking the safe and predictable road, doing what I'm supposed to do even when it doesn't feel right." She hesitated, then gave a small, wry smile. "If I were ice cream, I'd be vanilla. Plain, simple, expected."

MJ arched a brow. "Nothing wrong with vanilla."

She glanced up at him, something playful flickering in her eyes. "Maybe not. But there comes a time in a person's life when they just want to add some colorful sprinkles to that plain vanilla ice cream."

He chuckled, shaking his head. "So what you're saying is… you're ready to shake things up?"

She shrugged. "I don't know. Maybe. I just know I'm tired of always choosing the same thing because it's safe."

He leaned back, watching her for a long moment. "Well, for what it's worth, I don't think you're as vanilla as you think."

Miriam smirked, taking a sip of her coffee. "And what makes you say that?"

He grinned, tapping his fingers on the table. "Because vanilla wouldn't have defied her mother and hopped into my truck this morning."

Her laughter was soft but real this time, and MJ found himself smiling, too. For the first time in a long while, he wasn't the only one longing for something beyond what had always been expected of them. And that thought? That thought was something he hadn't let himself have before.

As they stepped out of the Sandwich Shoppe, the cold air bit at Miriam's cheeks, but she barely noticed. The morning had gone by faster than she expected, and the easy conversation with MJ had left her feeling both lighter and more unsettled at the same time. She still wasn't sure what to make of him; of his ideas, his humor, or the way he seemed to see the world so differently than anyone else she knew.

MJ opened the passenger door to let her in. "I've got a little time before I need to be home for afternoon chores. Want to go to the library for a bit before I take you home?"

Miriam hesitated for only a moment before nodding. "*Jah*, I'd like that."

THE LIBRARY WAS quiet when they walked in, the smell of old books and polished wood greeting them as they stepped inside. Miriam peeled off her gloves, rubbing her hands together for warmth as she glanced around. The last time they were here, she had stumbled across MJ in the travel section.

Miriam found herself back in the same aisle she had browsed before, running her fingers along the spines of books about hiking, backpacking, and wilderness survival. But this time, she wasn't just skimming. She pulled one from the shelf, *A Beginner's Guide to Hiking*, and flipped through the pages, absorbing every word. The thought struck her suddenly: *Why am I reading this?*

At first, she had told herself she was just curious. But now, standing there in the library, a book about hiking in her hands, she knew it was more than that. She wanted to understand what it would mean to go beyond Willow Springs, beyond the world she had always known. Maybe not now, maybe not ever, but the idea of it… it was starting to take root.

Across the library, MJ wandered the aisles, but his mind wasn't focused on the books in front of him. He had meant to grab another guide on camping, maybe something on trail mapping, but instead, he found himself standing still, staring at the rows of books without really seeing them.

His thoughts kept drifting back to Miriam.

She had been different this morning; less guarded, more open in a way he hadn't seen before. The way she talked about feeling out of place in her own life, about wanting more than what was expected of her… it struck a chord deep within him. He'd spent years planning his escape, carefully saving, calculating how much longer he had to endure his father's expectations before he could take off.

But now, for the first time, he wondered what leaving would mean for her.

His hand slipped into his pocket, fingers brushing against the bank book he always carried. He pulled it out, flipping it open, somehow hoping the total had increased since the last time he looked at it.

Miriam wasn't part of his plan. She had never been. And yet, when he thought about walking away from Willow Springs, from the farm, from all of it… the thought of leaving her behind didn't sit right.

Shaking his head, he closed the bank book and shoved it back into his pocket. He had always known he was leaving. But now, for the first time, he wasn't so sure he wanted to go alone.

He glanced across the library, spotting Miriam absorbed in a book, her brows drawn together in concentration. A small smile tugged at the corner of his lips. She was trying to figure something out, just like he was.

Maybe they weren't so different after all.

THE TROYER FARMHOUSE was quiet except for the low murmur of voices coming from the kitchen. Evelyn stood at the sink, scrubbing dinner dishes with unnecessary force, her jaw tight with frustration. Bennie sat at the table, arms folded as he watched his wife work through her anger, knowing better than to interrupt just yet.

Finally, Evelyn turned, gripping the towel in her hands. "Well? What are you going to do about Miriam's defiance?"

Bennie sighed, rubbing his forehead. "What do you expect me to do? She's turning twenty-four tomorrow. She's not a child anymore."

"She may not be a child, but she is acting like one! Running off in that King boy's truck, defying me right in front of you, making a spectacle of herself!" Evelyn's voice trembled, whether with anger or something else, Bennie wasn't sure. "If we don't do something now, she'll ruin her reputation, for *sure and certain.*"

Bennie exhaled, choosing his words carefully. "Or"—he leveled her with a calm look—"if you press too hard, you'll push her right out of our lives."

Evelyn's mouth opened as if to argue, but Bennie continued, his voice gentle but firm. "You can't box her into a corner she can't get out of. You know as well as I do what happens when a person feels trapped. They'll find a way to escape. And if you make her feel like there's no room for her here, she might just decide to fly the coop for good."

Evelyn's shoulders stiffened, but she didn't immediately argue.

Bennie leaned back, his gaze distant for a moment. "I keep thinking about my mother. About all the things she wished she had seen before her eyesight got too bad. She used to sit by the window and talk about all the places she would have gone, the sights she would have taken in if she'd had the chance. I don't want Miriam to live with that kind of regret."

Evelyn turned back to the sink, gripping the edge as if steadying herself. "I just want what's best for her, I want her to be happy."

"Then let her live a little, let her breathe. If she's going to make a life for herself here, she has to feel like it's a choice, not a cage."

Evelyn was quiet for a long moment before finally nodding. "I don't like it."

Bennie smiled wryly. "I know. But trust me, being a parent of older *kinner* means knowing when to hold on and when to let go."

Evelyn sighed as she dried her hands on the towel. "You sound just like your mother."

"She was a wise woman, and if she were here, she'd tell you the same thing."

Evelyn huffed but didn't argue. Instead, she silently returned to her tasks, the conversation settling into the space between them as she stewed about how she would rein in her wayward child on her own.

CHAPTER 5

$\mathscr{M}$J lingered just outside the porch, his fingers curling around the package he had brought for Miriam. Laughter spilled from inside, warm and inviting, but it only made the cold feel sharper against his skin. He had come because Hannah had insisted, practically dragged him here with one of her well-placed glares and a "Don't be a stubborn mule" remark. But now that he was standing on the outskirts of it all, he wasn't sure why he had agreed.

Through the kitchen window, he could see the celebration unfolding. Miriam sat surrounded by her family. He watched as she smiled at something her father said, her eyes soft, her hands folded in her lap. She looked... content. And for a brief, irrational moment, he wondered if he was about to ruin that.

He had never been nervous about giving someone a gift before, but bringing a gift went against their Amish traditions. However, as he rolled the package between his fingers, doubt crept in.

The hiking backpack had been an impulse buy... well,

if you could call spending half an hour staring at it in the second-hand store before pulling out his wallet an impulse. The poles had come later, after he spent too much time thinking about how she'd actually use the pack. And the note… that was the part that unsettled him most.

Because what was he trying to say?

He had told himself it was just encouragement. That he had seen something in her, an untapped potential, the same restless curiosity he felt. But now, standing here, the gravity of that realization pressed down on him. Maybe it was more than that.

Maybe it scared him that he had found someone who made him question his well laid-out plans.

A gust of wind whipped through the yard, rattling the shutters and making him shiver. He inhaled deeply, trying to shake the unease settling in his chest.

You're overthinking it, MJ. Just go in, give her the gift, and be done with it. With a determined exhale, he knocked on the door.

THE HOUSE WAS FILLED with quiet laughter and the warm scent of Miriam's favorite carrot cake with orange frosting, a simple but cherished treat her mother made only once a year. The Troyers didn't believe in celebrating birthdays with gifts or parties, not the way the *Englisch* did, but Evelyn had always marked the day with a special dinner, inviting the family and preparing Miriam's favorite dishes. It was one of the few traditions she allowed herself to hold on to, even as she kept tightly to the *Ordnung* in every other way. Yet even in the comfort of familiar voices and clinking dishes, Miriam couldn't shake the weight of her mother's watchful eyes or the silent expectations that still hung in the air.

The atmosphere should have been joyful, and for the most part, it was. But the moment MJ stepped through the door, everything shifted.

Miriam didn't have to look to know her mother's expression had soured. She could feel it from across the room, the way she stiffened as she set the cake in the center of the table.

"*Ach*," her voice was tight as she turned to Miriam. "It seems you have a special guest tonight."

Miriam met her mother's gaze evenly. "Hannah invited him."

"Did she now?" she murmured.

Miriam sighed. She had known this would be an issue, but she had hoped her mother would let it go for one evening.

Her father must have caught the tension because he leaned toward her mother and whispered something in her ear.

Miriam couldn't hear the words, but she saw the way her mother's lips grew tighter before she turned away, muttering something about checking on the ice cream.

Hannah came up beside Miriam and nudged her elbow. "Ignore her," she whispered. "It's your birthday. Enjoy it."

Miriam forced a small smile and nodded, but the discomfort lingered.

As the evening went on, MJ kept his distance for the most part, chatting with her *bruders* and only catching her eye now and then. It wasn't until later, when the crowd had thinned and some of the younger children had dozed off in their mothers' laps, that he found her by the back door.

"Come outside for a minute?" he asked casually, keeping his voice low.

Miriam hesitated. "Why?"

"I've got something for you."

Curiosity won over hesitation. She grabbed her shawl and followed him out into the cold night air.

"Here," he crouched near the door. He pulled out a small, wrapped bundle from behind the wooden rocking chair and handed it to her. "I saw this at the second-hand store and thought you might like it."

Miriam's fingers brushed against the rough paper, her heart unexpectedly skipping a beat. "What is it?"

"Open it later. But when you do, just know there's more. I left something for you under your bedroom window, behind the bushes."

She raised a brow. "MJ—"

"It's not a big deal," he shoved his hands into his coat pockets. "Just… something I thought you'd like."

She held the bundle against her chest, warmth creeping into her fingers despite the cold. "*Denki.*"

He nodded once, then glanced back toward the house. "We should go in before your *mamm* notices you're gone."

Miriam let out a soft laugh, but as they turned back toward the house, the sting of her mother's earlier words settled over her like a heavy quilt.

"You shouldn't get involved with that boy," her mother had warned her in a quiet, clipped tone when no one else had been listening.

The words had cut deep, deeper than she wanted to admit. And now, as she glanced at MJ beside her, she couldn't stop the doubt from creeping in.

She had never let herself think about MJ that way before. But if she ever did… would her mother be right?

T<small>HE HOUSE HAD FALLEN</small> into silence, the laughter and conversation from her birthday gathering now just a memory. Miriam had slipped upstairs earlier in the evening to set MJ's gift on her bed, resisting the temptation to open it in the midst of her family's watchful eyes. But she had one more thing to retrieve before she could finally see what was inside.

She waited, listening carefully to the sound of her father's soft snores drifting from her parents' room. Only when she was certain the house was deep in slumber did she grab her flashlight and tiptoe downstairs. Each step on the polished wood was measured, her feet knowing exactly which boards would betray her with a creak.

The night air was crisp as she stepped onto the porch, pulling her sweater tight around her bed dress. The moon hung bright and full, illuminating the winter landscape with beauty. She moved toward the bushes beneath her window, her breath curling in the cold air.

Her fingers brushed against something smooth and cold. She crouched, reaching beneath the branches and pulling out two hiking poles, their metal gleaming under the moonlight. A warmth spread through her chest that had nothing to do with the shawl she clutched around herself. MJ had left these for her. He had thought of her.

Following her own footprints back to the house, she slipped inside, locking the door behind her before padding up the stairs. The warmth of her bedroom welcomed her, and she wasted no time turning up the lamp near her bed, curling cross-legged beneath her quilt with excitement bubbling up inside.

The brown paper wrapping crinkled as she untied the twine, unwrapping the package with careful fingers. Inside was a backpack, not just any backpack, but a hiking pack, well-loved and broken in, its fabric a mix of grays and blues.

At least, she thought it was blue, but wasn't sure. Colors were harder to discern now, fading into muted shades, their vibrance slipping away like the edges of a dream upon waking.

She ran her hands over the fabric, feeling the sturdy straps and the many pockets. What could a person possibly need to store in each of these compartments? Her fingers traced the zippers, curiosity growing as she explored its features. Then, in one of the front pockets, she felt a folded piece of paper.

A note.

She pulled it out, her heartbeat quickening as she unfolded the small, handwritten message: *Someday, I hope you step beyond what's familiar and get to experience the things dreams are made of. – MJ*

It was simple, direct, and undeniably MJ.

Miriam swallowed hard, rereading the words over and over, turning them over in her mind. She had spent so much of her life playing it safe, following the expected path. But here, in her hands, was something that whispered of possibilities beyond the four walls of her safe and predictable Amish world.

She traced the ink with her fingertip, her heart still trying to understand what he was hinting at. As she turned the light down, she carefully slid the gift under her bed, hiding it away like a secret she wasn't sure she was ready to share.

Could she really take on a hobby like hiking before her eyesight faded even more? The doctors had said it could be years before she needed more assistance, but the uncertainty weighed on her. What if she couldn't do something so bold? What if MJ's gift was just a kind gesture, not a challenge he actually thought she would accept?

Doubt curled within her, whispering that she was foolish for even considering it. Hiking wasn't something Amish girls did. It wasn't something *she* did.

But as she lay back on her pillow, pulling the quilt up to her chin, the questions wouldn't stop. She would talk to Hannah about it tomorrow. Maybe Hannah could help her make sense of it all.

For now, she closed her eyes and let sleep take her, dreaming of what the world might look like beyond Willow Springs, beyond the careful, confined life she had always known, and beyond the reach of her overbearing mother.

THE AIR inside the house hung heavy, as weighty and gray as the winter storm clouds lingering outside. Miriam had been up early, trying to keep herself busy, but there was no escaping the tension that had been brewing since the night before.

Her mother had been quiet all morning, her silence sharper than any words she could have spoken. But when she finally did break it, it was with a single question Miriam had been dreading.

"Are you going to tell me the truth about that King boy?"

Miriam stiffened, pausing mid-step on her way to the sink. "What truth?" She tried to keep her voice even, but she knew it didn't matter. Her mother already had her own version of the truth, and nothing Miriam said would change it.

Her mother turned from the stove. "I saw the way he

looked at you last night. And I saw the way *you* looked at him. Don't try to tell me it's nothing."

Miriam sighed, standing at the sink, letting her hands move over the warm water as she scrubbed a plate. "It *was* nothing. MJ and I are just friends."

Her mother arched a brow. "Friends? That's what you're calling it? And what will you do when he decides friendship isn't enough? When he realizes that—"

"*Mamm,* stop," she muttered as she scrubbed a stubborn spot on the pan she was washing. "Please. Not today."

Her mother scoffed. "Not today? And when, then? When you realize you have no place in his world, nor he in yours? You can't afford to be reckless, Miriam. You, of all people—"

Miriam pushed back from the sink abruptly, the warm water dripping from her fingers. "I don't need you to remind me of what I already know." The words came out sharper than she intended, her frustration boiling over. She turned too quickly as she reached for a dish towel, but her foot caught the corner of a wooden stool tucked just outside her central vision. In an instant, she was falling. Her hands shot out to brace herself, but she landed hard on her side, and a sharp, tearing pain shot through her shoulder. The impact rattled her bones, a cry escaping her lips before she could stop it.

Her mother gasped. "Miriam!"

A rush of footsteps followed, and before she could even fully process what had happened, her father was kneeling beside her.

"Don't move. Where does it hurt?"

Miriam swallowed hard, blinking against the pain spreading from her shoulder down her arm. "I think... my shoulder—" She hissed as she tried to shift. "I can't move it right."

Her mother hovered over them, her face pale. "She didn't even see it. She tripped because she *didn't see it.*" Her voice shook, and Miriam didn't have to look at her to know what she was thinking.

"We need to get her to the hospital," her father demanded, already rising to his feet.

Miriam clenched her jaw to fight the wave of doubt creeping in. This wasn't what it looked like. It was just an accident. It could have happened to anyone.

THE TROYER FARMHOUSE was eerily quiet when Miriam stepped inside, her arm wrapped in a sling, her shoulder aching with every movement. The ride home had been long, the pain medicine leaving her groggy and disconnected, but nothing dulled the weight pressing down on her chest.

She wasn't sure what she had expected when she walked through the door. Maybe some sign of warmth or concern. But the moment her mother turned from the sink, drying her hands on a dish towel, Miriam knew exactly what was coming.

"Well," she huffed, eyeing her from head to toe. "That didn't take long."

Miriam frowned, shifting awkwardly as she tried to remove her coat one-handed. Her father reached to help, but she stiffened, not wanting the attention. The last thing she needed was to feel more helpless than she already did. "What didn't take long?"

"For you to prove what I've been saying all along," her mother replied, folding the towel with slow, deliberate movements. "That you aren't careful enough. That you don't pay attention to your surroundings.

Miriam swallowed hard. She had told herself she wouldn't let her mother's words get to her.

"*Ach*, it was just a fall." Miriam's father's voice was firm but tired. "Not the end of the world."

Her mother shot him a look but didn't argue. Instead, she turned back to Miriam, her lips pursed. "And what if it had been worse? What if you had broken your arm instead of just popping your shoulder out of place? What if next time, you hit your head? What if next time, you can't get up at all?"

Miriam clenched her jaw. "There doesn't have to be a 'next time.' It was just an accident."

Her mother let out a heavy sigh and shook her head. "You think it was just an accident, but it's not, Miriam. It's a pattern of not seeing what's right in front of you. And it's only going to get worse. If you can't see what's at your feet in your own home, how do you expect to manage anywhere else?"

Miriam exhaled sharply, biting back a response. Her shoulder throbbed, her body exhausted, but the battle between them wasn't one she could walk away from.

Her mother crossed her arms, her eyes narrowing as if she could see into Miriam's very thoughts. "This should be a wake-up call for you. Maybe now you'll listen. Maybe now you'll accept that the life you've been imagining for yourself isn't possible. That it's time to stop pretending you can do everything on your own."

Miriam stiffened. "I'm not pretending anything. I just want to be able to—"

"To what? Run around with a man who has no plans to stay in this community?" Her mother's voice sharpened, her hands pressing against the counter. "You think MJ will wait around when he realizes how much work you'll be?"

Miriam's breath caught in the back of her throat. Her mother wasn't just talking about her condition; she was predicting her future.

Miriam shook her head, heat rising to her cheeks. "*Mamm*, MJ and I are *just friends.* You're making a big deal out of nothing."

"Nothing? A young man doesn't take you out for coffee and come to a birthday party for nothing."

"I'm allowed to have friends, aren't I?"

Evelyn's eyes darkened. "Friendship has a way of turning into something else. And when it does, you'll see that I was right all along. Besides, young girls aren't just friends with young men in our community. It's not how it's done."

It didn't matter how many times Miriam told her mother the truth. She had already made up her mind. And that's what stung the most.

Her father's voice cut through the tension. "Evelyn, enough."

Her mother exhaled, exasperated. "*Nee*, Bennie. It's not enough."

Miriam bit her bottom lip, trying to find the right words. "You don't get to decide what's possible for me, *Mamm*."

Her mother's mouth thinned. "I don't have to. Life will decide for you."

Silence thickened between them.

Miriam's pulse pounded in her ears as she forced herself to stand tall. "If I fail, I fail. But that's *my* choice to make."

Her mother's expression didn't waver. "And what if it's

not just you who fails? What if you pull someone else into it?"

Miriam flinched.

Her mother turned, stepping away from the counter. "You'll see. When reality catches up with you, you'll see."

She walked out of the kitchen without another word, leaving Miriam standing there, fighting back tears.

Her father sighed and shook his head, setting a fresh cup of coffee in front of her. His touch was warm on her good shoulder as he said tenderly, "Don't let her words settle in your spirit."

Miriam swallowed hard and nodded.

But as her father stepped away, the grip of her mother's words still clung to her. And for the first time in a long time, she wasn't sure how to shake them off.

CHAPTER 6

*M*J pulled his truck to a stop just beyond the curve in the road, cutting the engine before it could rumble up the quiet lane. No need to rile Evelyn Troyer before he even set foot on the porch.

The crisp February air hit hard as he grabbed the bag of books from the seat beside him and started up the snow-packed driveway. It had been nearly four weeks since Miriam's accident, and he figured she had to be going a little stir-crazy by now. The least he could do was bring her something to pass the time.

Still, he hesitated at the steps with no good reason to feel this way… uneasy, like he was stepping somewhere he shouldn't be. He had dropped off books for Miriam before, had exchanged plenty with her over the years. But this time felt different.

Maybe because he'd thought about her too much since their talk at the Sandwich Shoppe, or maybe because he had spent longer than he cared to admit picking out the books, choosing ones he thought would feed whatever curiosity had sparked in her about hiking, adventure, and the world beyond Willow Springs. And just maybe it was because, for the first time, he was starting to realize he didn't like the idea of her being trapped here any more than he liked the idea of himself being stuck.

Shaking off the thought, he knocked firmly on the wooden door. A few moments passed, and then it swung open, not to Miriam, but to Evelyn.

She took one look at him, and her mouth flattened. "You again."

MJ forced a polite nod. "I came to bring Miriam some books. I figured she might—"

"She's resting," Evelyn cut in, crossing her arms over her apron. "She's had enough excitement to last her for quite a while."

Something in her tone bristled against him. "I won't stay long. Just wanted to drop these off."

Evelyn glanced down at the books, her gaze unreadable. "Books, always books," she muttered under her breath. Then, sharply, "There's more to life than a few books can offer. You of all people should know that."

He frowned, gripping the canvas bag a little tighter. "I don't see the harm in learning new things."

"The harm"—her voice turned icily smooth—"is in giving someone false hope."

His stomach knotted, though he wasn't entirely sure why.

Evelyn shook her head. "Miriam doesn't need distractions right now. She needs to focus on what's real. What's in front of her." Her gaze waved over him, assessing, before she added in a voice too low and pointed to be anything but intentional, "She doesn't need to be chasing after things she'll never fully *see*."

MJ stilled. The way she said it. Not like a figure of

speech. Not like she meant 'see' in some metaphorical sense. No. It was something else.

Something about the way she held his gaze just long enough to make sure he'd caught it. A warning wrapped in a secret.

He didn't know what to make of it, but before he could press her, she stepped forward, pulling the door halfway closed behind her like a sentry guarding a gate.

"Listen to me. I know you mean well, but you need to stop coming around."

His jaw clenched. "Miriam and I are just friends."

Evelyn's smile was slow, almost pitying. "A man and a woman don't stay just friends forever."

The words hit him harder than he expected. He started to protest, to tell her that she was reading into something that wasn't there, but the truth was he wasn't sure anymore.

Instead, he exhaled through his nose, keeping his voice even. "I'll leave the books here." He brushed the snow from the wood before balancing the bag on the railing.

Evelyn didn't stop him, didn't say another word as he turned and made his way back down the drive.

But her gaze pressed against him, steady and unspoken, as she stood in the doorway like a silent warning.

When he reached the bend in the road where his truck was parked, he glanced back once, just in time to see the curtain in Miriam's bedroom window shift.

She had seen him, and the look on her face etched an empty cry deep in his heart. The moment hung between them, heavy with the sense that nothing was going to change.

~

Miriam stepped softly down the stairs, her sore shoulder making every motion slower than usual. She hadn't expected to find her mother hunched over the sewing chest, her hands buried deep inside as if she were hiding something.

But she had seen it. The familiar cloth bag. The one she knew didn't belong to her mother.

Her heart gave a sharp thud against her ribs.

"Was that MJ at the door?" Miriam asked, keeping her voice even.

Her mother stilled for half a breath before gradually straightening. The hesitation was slight, but Miriam caught it. When her mother turned, her expression was unreadable, but her fingers still curled tightly around the handle of the bag.

"He wasn't looking for you."

The lie was as brittle as winter branches snapping underfoot.

Miriam's gaze flickered to the bag. A shadow of silence stretched between them, thick and suffocating. She could play along. Let it go. Pretend not to see what was happening.

Or she could do what she had never dared before.

Deliberately, she stepped forward, extending her good hand. "I'll take that."

Evelyn's grip tightened. "There are better ways to spend your time than wasting it on things that will never—"

"Never what?" Miriam asked, her fingers still outstretched.

Her mother's lips tightened, but she must have seen something in Miriam's eyes. A quiet knowing. A warning.

Because this time, her mother didn't push.

With a sharp inhale, she let go. Miriam took the bag,

her fingers curling around the worn straps. It felt heavier than it should have, weighted with more than just books.

She turned without another word, climbing the stairs slowly but deliberately, her pulse thrumming beneath her skin. She didn't fight, didn't argue… just walked away.

She had seen the truth for what it was. Her mother was trying to keep her from MJ for *sure and certain*.

EVELYN STOOD at the kitchen sink, gripping the counter as if it were the only thing keeping her from crumbling. The silence Miriam left behind lingered longer than usual, thick and unmoving.

Evelyn had seen it in her daughter's eyes, the quiet defiance, the way she had taken the books without a word. This wasn't just rebellion. This was a warning that she had pushed too far this time.

Miriam was slipping away.

The thought made her stomach clench as she turned to the table where Bennie sat, watching her with that same accusing expression.

"You keep pushing, and you're going to push her right into MJ's arms."

Evelyn's lips tightened. "That boy has one foot in the world. You know it as well as I do. If she gets tangled up with him, she might never come back, and besides, she's already a member of the church. She'll be shunned, no doubt about it."

Bennie exhaled through his nose, rubbing a hand down his beard. "And what's worse to you? That she might leave, or that she might want to forge her own path in life?"

Evelyn turned away, gripping the edge of the sink. "I don't want her throwing away her future on a man who won't stay. Someone who's restless, who doesn't know what he wants. MJ King is not the kind of man who will give her a stable life." She pressed her fingers into the countertop, steadying herself. "She needs security... someone who can take care of her in the long run when she can't manage on her own anymore."

Bennie leaned back, his chair creaking. "And you think you can arrange that for her?"

Evelyn swallowed. "I spoke with Eli Shetler."

Bennie's head snapped up, his entire body going still. "Eli Shetler?"

"He's looking for a wife," she pressed on, needing Bennie to understand. "His *kinner* are grown, and he doesn't need a young woman to bear him more. He's got a quiet home on the edge of town. He won't require much of her considering her future limitations."

Bennie stared at her like she had just spoken pure nonsense. "Eli Shetler is pushing fifty."

"He would be good to her," Evelyn argued. "He's a kind man. Steady. And he wouldn't expect things from her she can't give. No *kinner* to raise, no heavy burdens, just companionship."

Bennie's nostrils flared, and his hands curled around the arms of his chair. "And what happens when he's gone?"

She blinked. "What?"

"What happens when Eli Shetler dies?" Bennie snapped, his voice sharp now, cutting through the tension like a blade. "He's an older man. Twenty years, thirty at most, and then what? Have you thought about that? You're so focused on securing her future that you're not thinking past it!"

Evelyn's throat tightened. "She would—"

"She would *what*?" Bennie demanded. "Be a widow at

fifty-five? Alone with no one to care for her because you were too afraid to let her find a real match? Someone who might stand beside her for a lifetime instead of leaving her to fend for herself down the road?"

Evelyn's fingers trembled against her apron. She had spent so long thinking about Miriam's future that she hadn't thought about what came after.

"She needs someone… settled, dependable… someone who won't expect too much from her," Evelyn whispered.

"And what if that someone isn't Eli Shetler?" Bennie shot back. His voice softened, but the weight of his words didn't. "What if it's someone you don't approve of?"

Silence stretched between them.

Evelyn turned back to the sink, gripping it hard, staring at her reflection in the window glass. She didn't have an answer.

Because she knew deep down… she wasn't just afraid of Miriam being alone. It was something totally different.

MIRIAM CLOSED her bedroom door behind her with a measured calmness. She took a slow breath, willing the tension from the encounter with her mother to fade, but it clung to her like a burr caught in the hem of her dress.

Mamm had lied. Miriam had known it before she even asked. The way her mother had held the library bag too tightly, the way her fingers had curled around the strap like she was trying to keep a secret.

Miriam crossed the room, settled onto her bed with the bag beside her, her pulse quickening as she opened it. A neat stack of books rested inside, their familiar scent of aged paper and possibility greeting her like an old friend.

She ran her fingers over the spines, her eyes skimming

the titles: *Winter Camping Essentials, A Guide to Pennsylvania's Best Hiking Trails, Hiking for Beginners,* each one a whisper of something more, something beyond the walls of her small, carefully controlled world.

And then she found it. A folded slip of paper, tucked between the pages of one of the books.

She hesitated only a moment before pulling it free, her fingers smoothing out the creases.

MJ's handwriting was unmistakable. Short, deliberate strokes, like a man who said what he needed to say and nothing more. She read.

Miriam,

Winter hikes are different. I took the Seneca Trail at Cook's Forest last week. I wish you could have been there. It was like the whole world was holding its breath.
Cold enough to burn your lungs at first, but after a while, it wakes you up. The trees out there are massive. Older than anything we've got around home. Some of them are so big you'd need a few people to wrap their arms around them. You don't see trees like that every day.
The trail winds along the ridge, and when you hit the clearing, you can see the whole valley stretched out below. Snow-covered, quiet, like something out of a postcard. The river cuts through it, dark against all the white. I stood there longer than I planned just looking.
Wish you could've seen it. I hope someday, you will. If not with your own eyes, then maybe through mine.

–MJ

She let out a slow breath as she stared down at the letter, her fingers smoothing over the rough edges of the page. The words danced in front of her, lingering in her mind longer than they should have.

"If not with your own eyes, then maybe through mine."

A lump formed in her throat, but she swallowed it down instantly. He didn't know the truth behind the words. How could he? She hadn't told him and had sworn Hannah to secrecy.

Anyway, this wasn't about him. It wasn't about the way his words made her chest tighten or the strange warmth that had settled in her stomach as she read them.

Nee. It was just excitement. That's all. His words didn't hold a secret meaning. They never had. It was MJ doing something thoughtful, and she was reading into it like a foolish girl who didn't know better. She let out a small huff, shaking her head at herself.

Of course, he didn't mean anything by it.

He had always been kind to her. He had always shared books, always taken the time to talk when their paths crossed. She wasn't anyone special. She was just… what? Hannah's best friend. His little sister's tag-along companion.

That was all.

And if she started imagining more, if she started believing that there was anything deeper behind his words, then she was setting herself up for a disappointment of her own making.

Miriam folded the letter and tucked it back inside the book. She wouldn't write back. Not yet. Not because she wasn't grateful, but because she didn't want to make more of this than it was.

She had let her excitement run away, which was dangerous. She wasn't an adventurer. She wasn't someone who could just up and leave. She had responsibilities here, a life rooted in tradition. She wasn't like MJ, restless, searching, always wanting more… or was she?

She'd continue to read the books, tuck the moments away, and remind herself of what she already knew. She was just Miriam Troyer. And MJ was just being kind. Nothing more, nothing less.

~

MIRIAM STOOD AT THE COUNTER, mashing the pan of potatoes so hard that her knuckles ached. Her mother stood across from her, arms folded over her chest.

"You had no right," Miriam hissed, her voice low enough to keep from carrying into the front room. "I won't sit through dinner and pretend this is normal."

Evelyn let out a sharp breath through her nose, as if she'd expected this argument. "You're twenty-four, Miriam. And with your condition—"

"My condition?" Miriam's stomach twisted, but she refused to let her mother see the way it unsettled her. "Is that what this is about? You think I need a husband to hover over me?"

"I think you need stability," Evelyn corrected. "And Eli Shetler is a good man. He's already raised a family. He has no need for more children, no expectations of you beyond simple, manageable housekeeping and companionship. He's kind, practical, and most importantly, he's willing to look past—"

"Past what?" Miriam snapped, stepping forward. "The fact that my own mother thinks I'm incapable of having a normal life? That you went behind my back and arranged this as if I'm some child who can't make decisions for herself? And what makes you think I don't want *kinner* of my own!"

Evelyn's tone softened. "You act as if I'm handing you over to some monster. Eli isn't forcing you into anything. He's simply coming to dinner. It would do you well to show some manners."

The sound of the front door creaking open made them both jump. Miriam turned to see her father stepping inside, shaking the cold from his coat. His eyes fell on them immediately, narrowing as he took in the tension.

"What's going on?" he asked, setting his hat on the peg near the door.

Miriam opened her mouth, ready to unleash everything at once, but her mother's voice cut through before she had the chance.

"Eli Shetler is coming for supper," Evelyn announced.

Bennie froze, his brow furrowing in confusion. Then, as realization dawned, his expression darkened. "You invited Eli here?" His voice was laced with something dangerous, something Evelyn should have heeded.

Evelyn squared her shoulders, her chin lifting defiantly. "He's a good man, Bennie."

"I don't care if he's the bishop himself." Bennie's tone was sharp. "You didn't think to ask Miriam before arranging this?"

Evelyn turned to her daughter, frustration in her eyes. "She's being stubborn. You know as well as I do that we have to think about her future. Eli has agreed to give her a secure home—"

"A secure home?" her father's voice rose, his face growing red. "What about love? What about what *Gott* wants for her? Have you thought about that?"

Miriam sucked in a breath. The words hit her harder than she expected.

Evelyn's lips parted, but whatever she had been about

to say was cut off by the sharp sound of knocking at the door.

For a moment, no one moved.

Evelyn looked between them, then softened as she reached for Bennie's arm. "Please," she whispered, "just be civil. For one night."

Bennie looked as if he wanted to argue, but instead, he exhaled sharply, shaking his head before moving toward the door. Miriam's stomach twisted as she followed behind, her body stiff with unease.

Bennie pulled the door open, revealing Eli Shetler standing on the porch, his hands folded in front of him. He was older than Miriam had remembered, his hair mostly gray, deep lines framing his mouth.

"Evening," Eli greeted, stepping inside. His gaze drifted to Miriam, his eyes assessing but not unkind. "Miriam."

She forced herself to nod.

Evelyn gestured toward the table. "Come in, Eli. Supper's ready."

Miriam's spine stiffened. The room seemed to shrink around her, every path to the door suddenly blocked.

THE SCRAPE of forks against plates filled the silence, the grip of expectation pressed down on Miriam so much that she had trouble swallowing. Hardly touching the food before her, she laid her hand across her stomach, tight with unease.

Eli, however, ate without hesitation, cutting into his roast chicken with the precision of a man who had done this many times before. When he finally set his fork down, he wiped his mouth, turned to Miriam, and spoke with unsettling bluntness.

"Your mother tells me you have some struggles with your eyesight."

The words hit like a slap. Miriam grasped her hands on her lap, trying to control an outburst. She hadn't even told MJ, but here sat a stranger, speaking about it as if it were casual dinner conversation. She could feel her father tense beside her, his silence a clear warning.

Eli, either unaware or uncaring, continued. "I won't pretend to know what that's like, but I do know what it means to lose something. My late wife was sick for many years before she passed. I took care of her through all of it. I understand what it means to need help."

Miriam's heart pounded.

Eli leaned back, as if settling in. "That's why I think we'd make a good match. I have no expectations beyond companionship."

A cold wave crashed through her, deep and unshakable. She had feared this would be humiliating… but this? This was worse than she had imagined.

It wasn't a proposal. It was a contract.

A binding agreement meant to tether her to a man who saw her as nothing more than a convenience. A warm body to fill the empty space in his home.

Her stomach churned violently at the thought of what companionship meant to a man like Eli Shetler. A man old enough to be her father. A man who had already lived the life she had barely begun to dream about.

Her throat closed around a swell of panic, and for a moment, she couldn't breathe. The room pressed in too warm, too small.

Her mother's voice—so smug, so certain—echoed in the back of her mind.

"You won't do better than this, Miriam. He's willing to take you as you are."

79

"*Take me?*" she thought, the very idea made her skin crawl.

She forced herself to meet Eli's steady gaze, though she wanted nothing more than to shrink away from him. "So, that's what this is?" Her voice came out tight, barely above a whisper. "A practical arrangement?"

Eli nodded, unfazed. "What else is marriage if not practical?"

Miriam's stomach churned.

She glanced at her mother, waiting for her to object, waiting for any sign that her mother saw how wrong this was. But she sat silent, her lips pursed, her eyes downcast.

And suddenly, Miriam saw it for what it was.

This wasn't about Eli Shetler.

It wasn't even about marriage.

It was about her mother's fear, raw, desperate, and dressed up as concern. If she could arrange a future for Miriam that asked little and promised stability, then *Mamm* wouldn't have to face the truth that her daughter might never fit the mold of a typical Amish woman.

Not because Miriam wasn't capable, but because her mother had already decided she wasn't.

It wasn't protection. It was acceptance.

A quiet way of saying, *This is the best you'll ever get, so take it.*

And that stung more than any rejection.

Miriam's pulse pounded in her ears. She had to get out of here. She set her napkin down and pushed back from the table.

"Excuse me," she murmured, her voice steady despite the storm raging inside her.

She didn't wait for permission. She didn't look back. She walked away from the table and the life her mother was trying to force upon her.

CHAPTER 7

The first light of dawn crept across the frost-kissed fields and into Miriam's bedroom window. She moved with quiet determination as she cinched the straps of her backpack, ensuring it sat snug against her shoulders. Inside, she had packed a water bottle, a small bundle of snacks wrapped in a cloth, and a folded notepad she had tucked inside at the last minute.

Her heart pounded, not from fear, but from the undeniable thrill of finally taking control of something in her life.

She grabbed her hiking poles from where they leaned against her dresser and took one last look around her room. The house was silent, and she hoped to escape the fallout that was bound to happen with her mother if she was caught leaving the house.

The evening before had been unbearable. Her mother's voice at her bedroom door had been thick with disappointment, calling her name, pleading for her to be reasonable, to come back to the table, to just think about Eli's offer.

Miriam had pressed her face into her pillow, unwilling to give her mother the satisfaction of a response.

But now, she wasn't going to spend another moment trapped in that house.

She slipped out of her room, stepping carefully over the creaky floorboards as she moved toward the staircase. Her fingers hovered over the railing, but she didn't grab hold of it as if she couldn't trust herself to make it down a simple set of stairs without hesitation. If so, what right did she have to walk into the woods alone?

The kitchen was quiet. No morning coffee brewing, no clatter of dishes, just an eerie, waiting silence. Miriam's chest tightened, but she shook it off, pushing through the back door with caution.

The winter air hit her cheeks, fresh and invigorating as she headed to the barn, its doors already dusted in the light of sunrise. She needed to move quickly, finish the chores before anyone could question why she was up so early.

Inside, the scent of warm hay and livestock was a comfort. She set her hiking poles against the stall wall and moved abruptly through the motions of making ten bottles of calf milk.

The calves greeted her eagerly, their pink noses nudging at the metal gates, small cries filling the quiet space. She murmured soft reassurances as she fed each waiting calf, working fast, her mind racing ahead to what lay beyond the line of white calf shelters.

Her mother's voice, sharp and insistent, tried to wedge its way into her thoughts.

"You can't afford to be reckless, Miriam."

She exhaled, shaking her head. Not today. Today was hers to escape the suffocating walls of her bedroom and spend the day in the one place that gave her a sense of purpose... the woods.

When the last calf had finished suckling, she wiped her hands on her apron and moved toward the barn door, pausing only to glance around one last time.

No one was awake yet.

She grabbed her poles, slung her backpack higher on her back, trying not to notice the soreness in her still-healing shoulder and its limitations, and stepped outside into the full embrace of the morning.

The frozen ground crunched beneath her boots as she crossed the barnyard and slipped through the thin break in the trees where the path began.

This was her place. The one space untouched by everything else: her mother's expectations, the weight of her failing vision, the world's quiet insistence that she fit neatly inside its lines. The trees stretched tall and bare, their branches weaving a lacework of shadows on the ground.

As she moved deeper into the woods, the weight in her chest began to loosen.

Here, she wasn't the girl her mother pitied, the daughter being pawned off to a man she didn't want. She was just Miriam, a young girl with dreams of her own.

She pressed forward, stepping cautiously over exposed roots, gripping her hiking poles just a little tighter. The trail ahead stretched like an open invitation, winding through the trees toward a morning that belonged entirely to her.

The air was crisp, the essence of damp earth and pine, thick in the stillness of the morning. Miriam breathed it in, adjusting her grip on the hiking poles. The path ahead was well-worn, but her eyes weren't as sharp as they used to be.

She had spent so much time indoors these past few weeks, forced into rest while her shoulder healed. Her body ached for movement, for the freedom of being out in the woods again.

The trail curved ahead, dipping into a shallow ravine where the morning frost still clung to the undergrowth. She planted one hiking pole in the frozen dirt for balance and moved carefully down the incline. The ground beneath her boots was uneven, with thick roots cutting across the trail. She lifted her foot to step over one, but before adjusting, her toe caught on something she hadn't seen.

She lurched forward, her heart leaping to her throat.

Reflexively, she thrust her weight onto the hiking poles, digging them into the dirt. The solid grip saved her from hitting the ground, her balance wavering, but holding.

She exhaled shakily, her pulse hammering.

For a moment, she just stood there, gripping the poles tightly. If she hadn't had them… if she had fallen again… the thought sent a shiver down her spine.

It had been a small misstep, but it was a reminder; one she couldn't ignore. No matter how much she wanted to pretend otherwise, she wasn't like the other girls her age. And whether she wanted to admit it or not, there would come a day when she would have to rely on others in ways she wasn't ready for.

With a deep breath, she steadied herself and continued walking. The wind rustled through the bare trees, and ahead, the sound of careful footsteps echoed along the path.

Miriam slowed her pace as she spotted someone up ahead. An older woman in a fleece-lined jacket and a leather backpack slung over her shoulder. She carried a walking stick, her steps steady as she moved along the well-worn trail.

Miriam hesitated. She rarely ran into anyone out here.

As if sensing her presence, the woman turned. A friendly smile spread across her weathered face.

"Well, good morning," she greeted. "Didn't think I'd see anyone else out here this early."

Miriam offered a small smile in return. "I walk here often. My father's farm is just over the ridge."

The woman nodded approvingly. "Good place for it. I've been walking these trails for years." She tapped her walking stick against the ground. "My late husband and I hiked all over the country before he passed." The woman took a moment to look out over the woods ahead before adding, "It's a funny thing, when you've seen so many places, you always look for the next adventure. Today, I'm working on getting my trail legs back in shape to walk the Foothills Trail in South Carolina."

"Where have you traveled?" Miriam asked.

The woman's eyes lit up. "We spent most of our lives exploring. National parks, the Appalachian Trail, little tucked-away spots that most people never bother to see. We even took a trip to Spain and hiked some of the Camino de Santiago. Some of the best places are the ones you stumble upon by accident, but that trip was by far my favorite."

Miriam studied her, something stirring deep inside.

This woman had lived the kind of life Miriam never knew was possible.

"What about you?" the woman asked, tilting her head. "What do you dream of seeing?"

Miriam hesitated, suddenly feeling exposed to her lack of experience. What did she dream of seeing? The mountains? The forests? The endless trails that stretched beyond the world she knew? She had never been asked that before.

She swallowed, staring down at the frozen ground beneath her boots. "I... don't know. I guess I want to see what's beyond the twenty-five miles I've been contained to my whole life."

The woman smiled knowingly. "What do you want to see first?"

Miriam exhaled, her grip tightening on the hiking poles. "I'm not sure. Besides, I doubt I'll ever get the chance,"

The woman's expression softened. "Now, that's no way to be. Everyone needs adventure, and if they want it bad enough, they'll find a way." The woman waved her hands in front of her and looked ahead along the path. "God created all of this for us to enjoy. Who wouldn't want to see it all?"

Something inside Miriam broke loose. She had spent so much time thinking about what she couldn't do. What if, for once, she started thinking about what she could?

The woman gave her a parting nod before continuing down the trail, her steady steps carrying her away.

Miriam watched her go, feeling something new settle inside her as she looked for a place to sit and rest.

Miriam didn't stop walking until she found the perfect place. The fallen log nestled near a bend in the trail where she and Hannah hid their treasures. The clearing was quiet, save for the occasional rustle of wind through the trees as she pulled the glass jar from its hiding place. She pulled out her last hidden message and read it out loud... *"I promise to live life fully, no matter what!"*

She tucked the note back in the jar and pulled her notepad from her backpack. For a long moment, she just held the pencil in her fingers, staring at the blank page.

Then, slowly, she began to write.

MJ,

I wasn't sure if I was going to write back, but as I walked the trail today, I kept thinking about your last letter, about how you described the way the winter light hits the trees, how the snow crunches underfoot, how the wind moves through the evergreens. I tried to see it all through your eyes, the way you would.

And you were right. It's different when you really stop to look.

I've walked this trail more times than I can count, but today, it felt new. Maybe because I was paying attention in a way I hadn't before. Maybe because for the first time, I realized how much I still want to see.

I need to warn you that coming to the house isn't a good idea anymore. My mother won't allow it, and I don't want you to have to deal with her disapproving glares or worse, her words. If we're going to keep exchanging books, we'll have to find another way.

I'm leaving this letter in your truck, but maybe you can think of a better place to swap books and notes? Somewhere safe, where no one else will question it.

I just want you to know that I value your friendship. More than you probably realize.

Right now, what I need most is a friend who sees the world the way I do. Someone who understands what it's like to wonder if there's more beyond what we've always known.

Your friend,

Miriam

Miriam folded the letter gently, smoothing the creases with her fingers before tucking it back into her backpack. She pulled the zipper closed, ensuring the note was safe until she could slip it into MJ's truck unnoticed.

Leaning back against the fallen log, she reached into her bag and pulled out a small cloth bundle, unwrapping the simple snack she had packed that morning: a soft pretzel and a few slices of cheese. She wasn't terribly hungry, but she forced herself to take a bite, chewing unhurriedly as she listened to the forest around her.

For a moment, she let herself breathe in the solitude. Out here, there were no disapproving glances, no whispered worries about her future. Just the trees, the sky, the steady rhythm of her own heartbeat as she sat in the quiet.

With a satisfying sigh, she dusted the crumbs from her lap, packed away the remains of her snack, and slung her backpack over her shoulder. The weight had shifted, no longer just books and water, but something more… the letter she'd tucked inside. A piece of herself, folded into words meant for MJ alone.

Adjusting her grip on her hiking poles, she stepped back onto the narrow trail. She moved steadily, careful with her footing, thankful again for the support of the poles when she stumbled over a hidden root.

The path curved gradually downhill, leading her toward the back edge of the King farm where MJ's truck sat tucked between the trees, hidden out of sight from anyone who might question its presence.

As she neared, her steps slowed, and she glanced over her shoulder, ensuring she was alone. The farm was quiet, no movement near the barn or house. Taking a final steadying breath, she slipped toward the truck, her heart hammering a little faster than she liked.

Cautiously, she reached for the door handle, opened it just enough to slide her letter inside, and placed it beneath a book he had left on the passenger seat.

With one last glance around, she stepped back, shutting the door as quietly as she could.

And then, without a second thought, she turned and walked away. Back toward home. Back toward the uncertainty of what lay ahead.

~

MJ LEANED against the barn door, arms crossed, as he observed the shimmer of sunlight catching on something metallic. His sharp eyes tracked the movement as Miriam stepped cautiously toward his truck, glancing over her shoulder before slipping something inside.

But he remained still, melting into the shadows of the barn's overhang. His breath caught in the morning air as he watched her retreat, her steps sure but unhurried.

A slow smile pulled at the corner of his lips as he took in the sight of her. The backpack he had given her was strapped securely over her shoulders, and the hiking poles clicked lightly against the ground as she moved. She was using them.

That realization settled somewhere deep in his chest, unexpectedly warm.

He waited, watching as she disappeared beyond the treeline, her form swallowed by the woods that stretched between their farms. Only then did he push off the barn and make his way toward the truck.

The crisp air was already warming, soft drips of melting frost falling from the barn's eaves and splattering against the ground. His boots crunched against the packed earth as he approached the passenger's side door and opened it with a firm tug.

There, beneath the book he had left on the seat, was a folded piece of paper.

His pulse gave a strange, uneven kick as he picked it up and unfolded it. He scanned the words, his smirk fading into something quieter, more thoughtful.

Miriam's handwriting was neat, and her letters were beautifully formed. She was seeing the world through his eyes. Something about that made his chest tighten. He leaned against the truck as he reread the part where she mentioned finding a better way to exchange books. She

89

admitted she needed a friend who saw the world the way she did now.

Not just books. Not just notes. Understanding.

That's what she was looking for.

And maybe—just maybe—that's what he was looking for too.

Folding the letter, he tucked it into his jacket pocket and tapped his fingers against the truck's door, thinking.

A new exchange spot. He had an idea. And if she was willing to meet him halfway, the only problem was how he would let her know of his plans. He'd have to rely on Hannah for *sure and certain*.

MJ FOUND Hannah in the barn, brushing down one of the older workhorses. The rhythmic sound of the brush against the horse's thick winter coat filled the quiet space, the whiff of hay mingling with the cool dampness of melting frost outside.

He leaned against a wooden post, crossing his arms. "Need a favor."

Hannah arched a brow without looking up. "Let me guess… Miriam?"

He smirked. "You're good."

"I'm not good. You're just predictable." She set the brush aside and turned to him. "So, what is it?"

MJ reached into his coat pocket and pulled out the folded letter Miriam had left in his truck, smoothing it between his fingers. "She left me this. She wants to keep exchanging books, but we can't risk her mother finding out."

Hannah shook her head with a knowing grin. "So, you two are at last making sense of whatever this is?"

MJ shot her a look. "It's not like that."

Hannah snorted. "*Jah?*"

He ignored her, rolling the letter between his fingers. "She asked for a place where we could exchange books and notes, somewhere safe, where her mother won't catch on."

Hannah folded her arms. "And you want me to help how?"

"I think I found the perfect place. You remember the creek bend just past the property line?"

Hannah nodded. "The one with the big hemlock hanging over the water?"

"That's the one." He leaned forward, his voice low. "A few years back, I buried an old cooler out there. Just messing around as a kid, trying to make a secret storage spot. It's still there. Watertight, sealed up good. If I clear it out and cover it with the big hemlock branch, it'll stay hidden."

Hannah's brow furrowed. "You buried a cooler in the woods?"

He shrugged. "Had to keep my contraband root beer stash somewhere."

She snorted. "Unbelievable."

"But it's perfect," he insisted. "Hidden, weatherproof, close enough that Miriam can get to it but far enough that no one will notice her slipping away."

Hannah tapped a finger against her chin. "That could work."

"Tell her where to find it. I'll check it every few days. If she needs to send something back, she can leave it there."

Hannah gave him a long, considering look. "You're putting a lot of effort into this."

He shifted, glancing toward the barn door. "She needs a friend." His voice was quieter now, more certain. "So do I."

Hannah sighed, shaking her head with a small smile. "Alright, alright. I'll pass the message. But you owe me."

"I'll buy you a sticky bun next time I'm in town."

She rolled her eyes. "You're ridiculous."

However, as she walked away, something settled quietly inside MJ. The exchange was set. Now, it was up to Miriam.

CHAPTER 8

Miriam sat on the edge of her bed, the worn quilt bunched in her fists as she stared down at the letter MJ had hidden inside the book she had picked up that morning from their secret exchange spot. The words on the page blurred as she reread them, her heart pounding with each word.

> Miriam, I don't think I can stay here. I don't know what that means for me yet, but every day, I feel more certain that my future isn't here. I keep trying to ignore it, but it's always there, gnawing at me. I don't want to leave behind everything I've ever known, but I also don't know how to stay. I don't know why I'm telling you this, except that out of everyone, I feel like you might understand.

Her fingers tightened around the page, her chest constricting. She wasn't sure what she had expected when she picked up the book that morning, but it hadn't been this.

MJ wasn't just restless. He wasn't just different from the

other men in their community. He was admitting, in plain words, that he might not stay following his Amish roots. And that terrified her.

She had told herself for weeks that their friendship was nothing more than that. That the books, the letters, the hidden moments were all just part of a simple connection between two people who saw the world a little differently. But this letter changed everything. Because now, she couldn't pretend that this didn't have consequences.

Her mind spun a hundred thoughts all at once. If he left, what would that mean for her? He had never asked her to step out with him, never even hinted at it, but the thought of losing him entirely sent an ache through her chest. She shook her head, trying to push the thought away. He wasn't hers to lose. He never had been.

A creak in the hallway made her jump. She stuffed the letter under her pillow just as the door swung open. Her mother stood in the doorway, a laundry basket balanced on her hip, her sharp eyes scanning the room.

"I need your sheets," she hissed, stepping inside without waiting for permission. She moved to the bed, pulling at the quilt. "I want to get them on the line before we start dinner."

Miriam barely had time to react before her mother yanked back the pillow and froze. The letter, stark and undeniable, lay exposed against the mattress.

For a moment, there was silence. A heavy, suffocating silence. Then, deliberately, her mother reached down and picked up the folded paper.

Miriam's breath caught. "*Mamm—*"

But her mother had already unfolded the letter, her eyes scanning the words. The moment she reached the part about MJ not staying, her face darkened.

Her hands trembled, but her voice was cold as ice. "So. This is what you've been doing?"

Miriam opened her mouth to respond, but her mother's fury crashed over her before she had the chance.

"You've been sneaking around, exchanging letters with a boy who doesn't even know where he belongs?" Evelyn's voice rose, sharp and biting. "And you think this is acceptable? That *he* is acceptable?"

Miriam's stomach twisted. "*Mamm*, it's not like that—"

"Not like what?" Her mother snapped, waving the letter in the air. "Not like you've been lying to me? Not like you've been keeping secrets under my own roof?" She took a step closer, her eyes blazing. "You think you can build a future with someone who doesn't even know if he wants to be stay true to his heritage?"

Miriam recoiled. "I never said that."

"You didn't have to," her mother hissed. She held up the letter as if it were something dirty. "This is exactly why I told you to stay away from him. He's not stable! He doesn't belong in this life, and he knows it. And if you keep this up, you'll be the one left behind, broken-hearted, when he walks away."

The words sliced through Miriam, hitting every buried fear she had tried to ignore.

She had known MJ was restless. She had known he wasn't like the other men in their community. But seeing it in writing, knowing he had admitted it out loud, made it impossible to ignore. And now, her mother's voice only drove those doubts deeper, carving sharp lines where her certainty used to be.

Miriam straightened, lifting her chin despite the way her hands shook. "He's my friend. That's all."

Evelyn scoffed. "No, Miriam. That's *not* all. You may be too innocent to see it, but I'm not. He's a man who'll never stay put. And when he leaves, he'll take every foolish dream you've built with him."

Miriam's throat tightened. She wanted to fight back, to tell her mother she was wrong, but the truth was, she wasn't sure *what* was right anymore.

"No more letters. No more books. No more secret meetings. Do you understand me?"

A lump formed in Miriam's throat. What choice did she have?

Her mother exhaled, then turned on her heel, letter still clutched in her hand. "I won't let you throw your life away for a boy who can't even promise you one."

As the door slammed shut behind her, Miriam sat frozen, staring at the empty space where her mother had stood.

The pages of MJ's letter still burned in her mind, but now, they weren't just words. They were a warning. And maybe, just maybe, this time her mother was right.

MJ WIPED the sweat from his forehead with the back of his sleeve, adjusting the weight of the heavy feed sack on his shoulder before tossing it onto the growing stack in the back of a customer's truck. The morning sun had finally burned through the lingering chill, and the scent of grain mixed with the earthy smell of hay and sawdust.

He stepped back, nodding at the *Englisch* farmer waiting by the driver's side. "That should be all, Mr. Harper."

The older man adjusted his cap and gave a quick wave before pulling out of the loading zone, his tires crunching over gravel. MJ exhaled, rolling out the tension in his shoulders before reaching for the next order slip.

Then, a familiar sound, a buggy slowing to a stop.

MJ froze, his fingers gripping the paper a little too tight as his stomach clenched. He didn't have to turn around to know who had just arrived.

Evelyn Troyer's presence had a way of sucking the warmth out of the air before she even opened her mouth.

"Marvin J. King," her voice cut through the air, sharp as a blade.

He turned sluggishly, bracing himself for what was coming. She sat stiff-backed in the buggy, the reins gripped in one gloved hand, her other hand resting on her lap, fingers curled like she was trying to keep them from tightening into fists.

"Evelyn," MJ greeted evenly, pulling off his work gloves and tucking them into his back pocket. "What brings you to town?"

"I had errands to run. But I saw you out here and decided to stop. We need to have a talk."

MJ didn't have to guess what this was about. He glanced toward the store, debating whether to end this before it started, but Evelyn's sharp stare pinned him in place.

"I know you've been writing to Miriam."

His jaw tensed. He had suspected her mother would find out eventually, but it still set his pulse ticking faster. "I'm not sure what you mean."

Her brows arched. "Don't play dumb with me. I raised eleven *kinner*. I know when someone's sneaking behind my back."

He folded his arms over his chest. "Then I assume you also know Miriam's an adult, capable of making her own choices."

Evelyn let out a short laugh, one with no humor. "Capable? You think you know my daughter?" She leaned closer, lowering her voice. "Tell me, MJ… did she ever tell you why we worry about her?"

A sense of unease tightened in his chest. "Miriam's told me plenty."

"But not everything." Evelyn's gaze locked onto his, something unreadable in her eyes. "Do you know what's coming for her?"

His stomach twisted. "What are you talking about?"

She exhaled sharply, shaking her head as if he were a child too naïve to understand. "Never mind… it doesn't concern you. Just know she needs someone who can truly care for her."

His breath caught, his mind scrambling to make sense of what she wasn't saying.

Evelyn's mouth curved in satisfaction at his silence. "She doesn't need someone like you. Someone who's already got one foot out the door. Miriam needs a man who will stay, who will care for her when she can no longer care for herself. Someone who won't run when life gets too difficult."

He flinched, but she wasn't finished.

"You've spent years resenting the responsibilities laid at your feet. You think you're trapped, but you don't know the first thing about being trapped," she added. "You talk about seeing the world, about leaving, but what happens when you do? What happens when you get tired of small-town life, and Miriam can't keep up? You'll leave her behind, just like you've always planned to leave everything else."

A cold rage simmered beneath his skin. "You don't know anything about me."

"I know enough." She straightened her shoulders, steel in her voice. "You will break off all contact with my daughter. No more letters. No more books. No more secret meetings. Do you understand me?"

MJ's jaw tightened so hard it ached. He should have expected this. He should have known Evelyn would never approve.

But what he hadn't expected was the sharp pain pressing against his ribs, the deep, cutting realization that he hadn't just been writing to Miriam to give her books or talk about hiking.

He cared. More than he had wanted to admit.

Evelyn studied his face, seeming to find whatever answer she was looking for. She nodded, her victory all but claimed, and picked up the reins.

But before she could go on her way, MJ's voice cut through the air.

"You're wrong."

Evelyn paused, turning back toward him, her expression flashing with irritation. "Excuse me?"

"You're wrong about Miriam." MJ took a step forward, anger tightening his chest. "You think she needs protecting, that she needs a man to oversee her like she's some fragile thing. But I see her more clearly than you do. She doesn't want someone to keep her, she wants someone to walk beside her."

Evelyn's lips thinned. "You think she can do that alone? You think a woman will be fine without someone strong enough to support her?"

MJ shook his head, his jaw clenched. "I think you don't understand your own daughter."

Evelyn sighed, slapping the reins. "This is exactly why you are not the man for her."

MJ stood there long after she had disappeared down the road, Evelyn's words looping through his mind over and over again.

He had spent so much time thinking about his future, his need to escape, that he had never stopped to think about what Miriam was facing.

And now? Now, he needed to see her. Not to argue. Not to demand answers. But because, for the first time, he understood that his choices weren't just about him anymore.

BENNIE WATCHED as his daughter picked at her food, her usual appetite diminished to nothing more than slow, distracted bites. The soft clink of her fork against the plate was the only sound she made during the entire meal. Her shoulders were drawn tight, her expression distant. It hadn't escaped his notice that, for the past few nights, she had excused herself early, retreating to her room rather than joining the family in the front room as she always had before. He had let it pass once or twice, but tonight, the heavy silence hanging over the table gnawed at his patience.

Evelyn, on the other hand, acted as though nothing was amiss. She sipped at her tea with calculated ease, as if she couldn't feel the undercurrent of tension suffocating the room. Bennie set his fork down with a quiet sigh. "Miriam, are you feeling alright?"

Miriam blinked, as if pulled from deep thought. She hesitated for a moment too long before answering, her voice softer than usual. "I'm fine, *Datt.* Just tired."

Bennie wasn't convinced, and from the way Evelyn's shoulders stiffened, he suspected she knew more than she was letting on. "You've been quiet these past few days. You spend all your time in your room. I can't help but notice something's weighing heavy on you."

Miriam's fingers toyed with her napkin. She avoided his gaze and forced a small smile. "I've just had a lot on my mind."

Evelyn made a sound low in her throat, a noise that didn't quite qualify as a word but held plenty of meaning nonetheless. Bennie turned to his wife, his eyes narrowing. "What is it?"

Evelyn took another slow sip of her tea before setting the cup down carefully. "It's nothing. Just the troubles of a young girl getting ahead of herself. Nothing you need to concern yourself with."

Bennie's patience thinned. "I'll decide what concerns me. What have you done now?"

Evelyn drew herself up. "I only did what any good mother would do. I tried to prepare her for reality... what I've been trying to do all along with no help from you, I might add."

Miriam's grip on her napkin tightened as she cast her gaze downward.

Bennie's jaw went rigid. "And what exactly does that mean?"

Evelyn lifted her chin, her eyes sharp with determination. "I've arranged for her to begin learning Braille."

The words hit Bennie like a hammer. He stared at his wife, unable to comprehend what she had just said. "You did what?"

Evelyn's voice was firm, unwavering. "She needs to be ready for what's coming. The doctors have said it, Bennie. Her eyesight is only going to get worse. She needs to learn how to function in a world where she won't be able to rely on what little sight she has left. She may not want to face it, but that doesn't mean we can ignore it."

Bennie's temper was scarcely held in check. "And did you think to discuss this with her? Or with me?"

"She needs guidance," Evelyn argued. "She's too caught up in foolish notions, going on walks through the woods, dreaming about things that will never be. She needs to be practical. If she doesn't start preparing now, what will she do when the day comes that she can't read a book at all? When she can't even walk those trails without someone leading her?"

Bennie turned to Miriam, whose face had drained of color. She looked small in her chair, her hands gripping the napkin in her lap like a lifeline. Her voice was barely a whisper. "*Mamm*, I don't need this. Not yet."

"Then when? When it's too late? When you're forced to accept it with no time to adjust?"

Miriam abruptly pushed her chair back, the scrape of wood against the floor breaking the heavy silence. "*Datt*, please. I'm fine."

Bennie turned to his daughter, noting the way her hands trembled a bit as she smoothed her dress. He noticed something hollow in her voice, something that didn't sit right with him. He knew Miriam, knew her heart, her spirit, and he could see it dimming right in front of him.

"This isn't fine."

Miriam swallowed hard, her gaze flickering toward her mother before she stepped away from the table. "I think I'll go to bed early."

Bennie watched as she turned and walked toward the stairs, her steps slower than usual, her shoulders tense. A deep ache settled in his chest as he looked back at his wife.

"You're breaking her." He leaned forward, his voice dropping to a sharp whisper. "And if she does, it will be because of you."

Evelyn ultimately looked away, the tension between them stretching thick and heavy as Miriam's door closing echoed through the house.

~

MIRIAM HEARD Hannah's voice drift up the stairwell, followed by the soft creak of approaching footsteps. She exhaled, bracing herself. She knew why Hannah was here.

A gentle knock sounded at her door before it cracked open. "Miriam?"

Miriam hesitated, debating whether to pretend she was asleep. But it was too late, Hannah had already stepped inside, shutting the door behind her. She sat at the foot of the bed, her expression lined with quiet determination.

"MJ wants to see you." Hannah's voice was calm, with an edge of expectation in it. "Tomorrow afternoon. At the meeting place. Three o'clock."

Miriam's stomach clenched. She swallowed and shook her head. "I can't."

Hannah frowned. "Miriam, don't do this. Just talk to him."

Miriam looked down, her fingers tracing a wrinkle in her quilt. "I don't think we should keep this up; it's not going to change anything."

Hannah's brows drew together. "But why? What happened?"

Miriam pressed her lips together, willing her voice to stay even. "I just think it's best if we go our separate ways."

Hannah didn't respond right away. She studied Miriam, searching her face for an answer that wasn't being spoken aloud.

"Miriam…" Hannah's voice softened. "You don't have

to do this. You care about him. And I think he cares about you too."

Miriam's throat tightened. "It doesn't matter."

Hannah let out a slow breath, but Miriam could tell she wasn't convinced.

At last, Hannah nodded, though reluctantly. "I'll tell him."

Miriam forced a small smile. "It's for the best."

But as she watched Hannah leave, a hollow ache settled in behind her ribs. If it was truly for the best, why did it feel so much like she was losing something she hadn't even allowed herself to want?

CHAPTER 9

MJ paced the length of the barn, his boots scuffing against the packed dirt floor. The familiar scent of hay and livestock usually settled his nerves, but not tonight. He couldn't shake the restless energy coursing through him. Every few minutes, he'd glance toward the door, waiting for the telltale crunch of snow beneath boots. Hannah had been gone longer than he expected. That wasn't a good sign.

He ran a hand through his hair, exhaling sharply. The past few days had been a mess, one thing piling on top of another. Miriam refused to answer his last letter. Evelyn ambushing him at the Feed & Seed. And now this, her shutting him out completely.

The sound of the door creaking open made him spin around. Hannah stepped inside, shaking the cold from her bonnet before pulling it off entirely. One look at her face, and his stomach sank.

"Well?" he asked, bracing himself.

Hannah hesitated, her lips pressing together before she spoke. "She doesn't want to see you, MJ."

His jaw tightened. He had expected as much, but hearing it still hit hard.

"I don't get it," he muttered, running a hand over his face. "Why won't she tell me what she's going through?"

Hannah sighed and stepped closer. "She doesn't want people to pity her."

MJ let out a frustrated breath, shaking his head. "This isn't about pity." He stopped and looked hard at his *schwester*. "You know, don't you?"

"I do, but Miriam doesn't want anyone else to know... I promised her."

Before he could respond, heavy boots thudded against the floorboards. Their father's voice cut through the tension. He pointed a calloused finger toward the barn doors. "That truck of yours... it needs to go."

MJ tried to keep his temper in check. "I parked it down the road like you asked."

"That's not the point," his father snapped. "It doesn't belong here. You don't belong here, not while you keep acting like you've got one foot out the door. If you're going to be part of this family, you need to start acting like it."

MJ's frustration boiled over as he threw his hands up. "Fine, maybe I should just make it easy for you and leave."

His father's face darkened. "If you leave, you'll be just like every other young man who throws away his heritage because the world out there looks easier. You think you're the first to want something different?"

MJ's chest tightened. "I don't think it's easier. I just think it's my choice."

His father scoffed. "No, your choice was made for you the day you were born into this family."

MJ's pulse hammered against his temples. "That's the problem. You don't see that I should get to decide my own future. Just like Evelyn is trying to decide Miriam's."

His father's eyes flashed. "That's different."

"How?" MJ snapped. "You think forcing me to stay is any different than Evelyn trying to marry Miriam off to some man she barely knows? You're both trying to control something that isn't yours to control."

The barn fell into thick silence. His father's jaw twitched. "This is about responsibility, Marvin."

MJ exhaled sharply through his nose. "No, *Datt*. This is about control. And I'm tired of everyone making decisions for me!"

His father studied him, and after a long moment, he shook his head. "You'll regret it."

With that, he turned on his heel and walked out, leaving MJ standing in the center of the barn, his breath coming in sharp, uneven bursts.

Hannah's voice was quiet but firm. "Do you really think leaving is the answer?"

MJ let out a short, bitter laugh. "I don't know, but I know staying isn't working either."

She frowned, arms crossed. "And Miriam? What about her?"

MJ's stomach twisted. "What about her?"

"She's struggling, and she doesn't need you disappearing on her too."

His jaw tightened. "I don't know what she wants from me. She won't talk to me, she won't let me in—"

"Maybe because she's scared." Hannah folded her arms, her expression unwavering. "She's trying to figure things out, just like you are. But you're so focused on what you want, what you need, that you don't even see how much she's hurting."

MJ clenched his jaw, looking away. He wanted to argue, to tell Hannah she was wrong, but deep down, he knew she wasn't.

And that was the worst part.

~

THE AFTERNOON SUN stretched light beams through the bare trees, warming Miriam's face as she stepped onto the familiar trail. The soft earth beneath her boots still held the damp chill of early spring, and she was grateful for her hiking poles as she navigated the muddier patches.

It had been weeks since she had taken a walk. Too many weeks of being cooped up inside, of restless nights and heavy thoughts that had nowhere to go. With her parents off visiting one of her older *schwester's* homes, she was free to breathe, to move, to exist in the peacefulness that the woods provided.

The forest had shaken off most of winter's hold. The trees were still mostly bare, their branches stretching skyward like bony fingers, but here and there, buds swelled with the promise of new life. A robin trilled somewhere nearby, its song breaking the stillness with a cheerful melody. The creek, swollen from melted snow, bubbled over rocks, making a beautiful melody.

Her boots scuffed against the muddy dirt as she made her way deeper into the trail, her body easing into the rhythm of movement. It was good... familiar. Like brushing against a part of herself she hadn't touched in a long time.

But even as she embraced the peace of the woods, her feet carried her toward the hidden cooler. She knew there wouldn't be anything waiting inside. Especially not after she had refused to meet MJ. He wouldn't have written again, not after she had made it clear they needed to part ways. Still, she found herself drawn there.

The hemlock branch covering the cooler was

undisturbed, the same as they had left it. She hesitated, then knelt, pushing the branch aside before prying the lid open.

Her breath caught.

Not only was there a new stack of books waiting inside, but several folded letters sat neatly on top. Her fingers hovered over the letters before she clenched them into fists. She had told herself she was done, that she couldn't afford to keep this up. But MJ had written anyway.

She exhaled sharply and snapped the lid shut.

Nee.

She wasn't doing this.

Without letting herself dwell on the disappointment, she turned and walked away.

The trail stretched before her, winding through the quiet woods. The sun had risen high overhead, turning the sky into a pale wash of blue. She walked, her mind churning, her heart at war with itself.

But a mile down the path, she stopped and turned back.

Without letting herself think too much, she retraced her steps, her feet moving with purpose. Within twenty minutes, she was back at the hidden spot, kneeling once more to retrieve what she had left behind.

She didn't open the letters. She didn't flip through the pages of the books. She simply tucked them away in her pack and started for home, her heart hammering with the urgency of getting back before her parents returned.

The thought of facing her mother right now made her stomach twist. She had always been able to find the bright side of things, to see *Gott's* hand at work even in difficult moments.

But now? Now, all she could see were obstacles. Doors

being shut. Choices being taken away. She didn't like what she was turning into.

Reaching the clearing where the King farm met the Troyer land, she stopped. The warmth of the afternoon sun kissed her cheeks, and she turned her face toward the sky, closing her eyes.

She let the rest of her senses take over.

The world around her was alive in ways she hadn't fully appreciated before. The air carried a thousand scents: the damp richness of the earth, the sweetness of budding trees, the faint smoke of someone's chimney in the distance. The breeze, gentle and cool, brushed against her skin, wrapping around her like a whisper.

The sounds filled the space where her eyesight was beginning to fail. Birds calling to one another in the canopy above, the steady murmur of the creek winding its way through the valley, and the distant rustling of a deer moving through the underbrush enlightened her senses.

Gott had truly given her more than just sight.

Suddenly, a gentle breeze swept over her, and something familiar reached her nose, a scent she hadn't expected.

Grain.

The distinct scent mixed with the subtle notes of hay and wood shavings, the smell of MJ's work jacket after a long day at the Feed & Seed.

Her eyes fluttered open, and she turned, expecting to see him standing close by. But he wasn't. Instead, he stood at the edge of the clearing, nearly a hundred feet away, his posture rigid, his hands stuffed into his coat pockets. He was too far for her to smell anything at all.

Her breath caught. It had been so vivid; like he had been standing right beside her. But he wasn't. A shiver ran down her spine, but not from fear.

Gott, is this You? Are You showing me that where my eyes fail, You will compensate with something else? That I don't have to be afraid?

Her heartbeat thundered in her ears. She and MJ simply stared at each other, a void of silence between them. She wasn't sure how long they stood like that. Seconds? Minutes? But then, just as gradually as he had appeared, he gave a small nod and turned away, disappearing back toward the barn.

Miriam's fingers tightened around her hiking poles as a quiet understanding settled over her heart. A lump formed in her throat, and she lifted her face to the sun.

Lord, I'm scared. I don't know what my future looks like, and I don't know how to move forward. But I don't want to lose myself in this fear. If You're showing me that I can still have a full life, even if it looks different than what I planned, help me to believe it. Help me to trust You.

Miriam opened her eyes, blinking against the brightness.

She took a deep, steady breath for the first time in weeks, feeling the weight on her chest ease just a little. But in that moment, she knew one thing for certain... *Gott* was trying to show her something.

MJ SHIFTED the worn leather strap of his hunting rifle over his shoulder as he stepped into the small pawn shop in the middle of town. The chime above the door banged, announcing his presence. The place smelled of old wood, metal, and dust, a combination of things long forgotten and those waiting for a second chance.

He had never liked hunting. Not really. The heaviness of the rifle in his hands had never brought him the same satisfaction it did his *datt* and *bruders*. To them, hunting was a necessity, a skill passed down through generations. But to him, it had always seemed like taking more than what was needed … an act that left something unsettled in its wake.

Still, he had gone along with it, just like he had with everything else expected of him. The long treks into the dense forests, the stiff hours spent crouched in wait, the smell of gunpowder mixing with the crisp autumn air… it had been part of the life mapped out for him, another piece of a puzzle he didn't quite fit into. But today, he was letting it go.

An older man with wiry gray hair and thick glasses perched at the counter glanced up as he set the rifle down. "What can I do for you?"

MJ exhaled, resting his hands on the glass case. "Looking to sell. I got a couple of rifles and a shotgun." He reached into his coat and laid down a box of shells alongside them. "Figure someone else might get better use out of 'em."

The man grunted, picking up the first rifle and giving it a once-over. "They're in good condition." He checked the barrel and the stock. "Don't see many Amish boys pawning their guns."

MJ smirked, though it lacked humor. "Guess I'm not like most."

The old man gave him a long look, then nodded. "I can give you a fair price."

MJ took the cash without hesitation, tucking the crisp bills into his wallet. Every bit counted. He was getting closer.

∾

A week later, in the calm of the King barn, MJ sat in the dim light of a lantern, a notebook spread open on his lap. The pages were filled with scribbled notes, half-formed plans, and lists of supplies he would need for his trip.

Tent. Sleeping bag. Water filter. Trail map.

He tapped the pencil against the page, his mind racing ahead. Ten days on the Foothills Trail. That was the plan. It would be his first real taste of freedom, a break from everything he had ever known. After that? He had no clue. But for the first time, not knowing didn't scare him.

A shuffling sound at the barn entrance made him glance up. His father stood there, framed by the moonlight, arms crossed over his broad chest.

"I heard from Abe Miller today."

MJ set his pencil down, bracing himself. "Oh?"

"He says you gave notice at the Feed & Seed."

MJ nodded, refusing to look away. "That's right."

"And what exactly do you plan on doing? You quitting everything, walking away from your responsibilities, what does that get you?"

MJ let out a slow breath. "It gives me a chance to figure out what I actually want."

"And you think you'll find that out in the world? Out there, where people throw away their values like yesterday's trash? We raised you to be better than that."

"*Nee.* You raised me to be what you wanted me to be. I need to find out who I actually am."

His father took a step closer, his voice dropping to a warning tone. "Running won't fix whatever you think is broken, *sohn.*"

MJ met his gaze, the burden of his decision settling deeper in his bones. "Maybe not. But staying here will break me in a way I can't come back from."

His father's eyes darkened with disappointment, but he

said nothing more. After a long pause, he gave a curt nod and turned on his heel, leaving MJ alone in the barn once more.

MJ's heart pounded. He couldn't turn back now.

This was it. The first real step toward freedom.

THE AIR WAS warm enough that Miriam didn't need her heavier coat. A soft breeze moved through the budding trees, carrying the scent of wet earth and wild onions. Birdsong filtered through the woods like a hymn, and though the sun filtered gently through the branches, her boots still sank slightly into the damp path.

She walked deeper than usual today, past the edge of the family land. She needed distance. From the house. From her mother's sharp words. From MJ's recent confession that he couldn't promise he'd stay. He hadn't said it with anger. Just quiet honesty. But it had shaken something loose inside her.

The guidebook he'd given her was tucked inside her apron pocket, worn from repeated readings. She stopped beside the tall pine tree just beyond the edge of her family's land. This spot was hers, the one place where no one shaped her, no one told her who to be.

She pulled the book from her pocket and flipped it open to a page she'd nearly memorized: *Beginner Training Tips for Long-Distance Hikes*. Her eyes skimmed the list: *Build stamina. Add weight gradually to the backpack. Learn how to use a compass.* She traced the edge of the page with her finger.

She didn't need anyone to know. Not yet.

Miriam pulled a folded scrap of paper from her other pocket. On it was a short list, written late at night when doubts were loud and dreams louder. *Walk three miles every other day. Research day trip hike locations. Check the bus schedule. Look for a hiking partner. Hannah?*

She didn't know if she'd ever leave Pennsylvania. But something in her spirit whispered that preparing for the possibility was enough. It wasn't about rebellion. It was about reclaiming something she hadn't realized she'd given away. Her own voice and the will to do something beyond her mother's expectations.

Miriam held her face to the sun and whispered, "Lord, You made me strong. Help me to remember that."

She stood, heart calm, shoulders lightened and tucked the paper back into her pocket.

The biting scent of burning paper filled Miriam's nostrils before she even saw the smoke. Her heart stuttered in her chest, a cold sense of dread creeping up her spine. She knew. Even before her feet carried her around the side of the house, before her eyes confirmed what her heart already understood... she knew.

The metal burn bin crackled and spat embers into the air, releasing a thick, gray smoke that curled toward the sky. She skidded to a halt, her breath catching as she stared at the charred remains of books curling in on themselves, their spines blackened beyond recognition. Pages flared and disintegrated, MJ's careful handwriting disappearing into ash. *"Neeeee..."*

The word screamed through her mind, but no sound escaped her lips. She didn't need to ask how her mother had found them, she had suspected something was coming when she had sent her to the neighbor's for sugar despite the nearly full container in their pantry. It had been a ploy, a way to get her out of the house just long enough for her

115

mother to do what she had always done, erase any part of Miriam's life that didn't fit within the walls she had built around her.

Miriam's fingers clenched at her sides, her nails digging into her palms as she took a shaky step closer. Her mother stood beside the burn bin, her arms crossed, watching the flames as if they were nothing more than a means to an end.

She stopped, her chest heaving with unspoken words, grief slicing through her like a blade. She wanted to scream, to reach into the fire and pull the letters free, to salvage whatever she could. But it was too late.

The wind shifted, blowing a cloud of ash toward her, and she squeezed her eyes shut against the sting. When she opened them again, her mother at long last looked at her, her face a mask of cold finality. No words were exchanged; none were needed. The message had been delivered loud and clear.

Without a word, Miriam turned on her heel and walked away. Not toward the safety of the only life she had ever known, but toward her room, toward her escape. She needed to leave.

HER MIND RACED as she pulled her backpack from its place in the corner, stuffing it with whatever she could fit: an extra dress, her Bible, a journal she had managed to keep hidden. She grabbed her hiking poles, slinging them over her shoulder before stepping back into the hall. She held her breath as she passed through the kitchen, half expecting her mother to be waiting, ready to stop her.

But she was nowhere to be seen. It was almost as if she had already written Miriam off.

Miriam didn't let herself hesitate. Slipping out the back door, she pulled the straps of her backpack tighter and set her feet toward the only place she could think to go. Hannah's.

She didn't know what she would say when she got there. She didn't even know if she could explain the burning ache in her heart, the hollow loss that swallowed every ounce of fight she had left. But she knew she couldn't stay here. Not anymore.

CHAPTER 10

$\mathcal{M}$iriam slowed her steps as she neared the King barn, the worn boards reflecting the fading afternoon light. She had intended to go to the haus, to ask Hannah if she could stay for the night, but the sound of voices made her stop short. She pressed herself against the wooden slats, holding her breath as she realized who was speaking.

"So that's it then? You're really leaving?" Hannah's voice was hushed, but Miriam could hear the tremor of emotion in it.

MJ let out a heavy sigh. "Jah. I can't keep pretending. I was never meant to stay here. I quit the Feed & Seed, sold my hunting guns, and I've got enough saved up to make it work."

Miriam swallowed hard, her fingers curling against the rough wood. He was really leaving.

"*Datt's* gonna be furious," Hannah murmured.

MJ let out a humorless chuckle. "When is he not upset with me?"

A brief silence settled between them before Hannah's

voice softened. "I just don't want you to go and regret it. No matter how frustrating *Datt* is, this is still your home. And... I know you and Miriam have gotten close. Are you sure you want to leave her behind?"

Miriam's heart pounded, a heat rising to her cheeks. Hannah didn't know she was standing just feet away, hidden by the shadows of the barn. She squeezed her eyes shut, willing her emotions into submission. This wasn't about her. MJ had made his decision.

"She has her own life to figure out," MJ paused for a moment. "She's made it clear I can't be what she needs. And she... she's better off without someone who doesn't know where he belongs."

Miriam bit her lip, a thousand thoughts swirling through her mind. He was leaving. And that meant she had to decide: would she let him go, or would she take her fate into her own hands?

Hannah sniffled. "Just... be careful, okay? I know you want to figure things out, but don't lose yourself trying. And write to me. If you don't, I swear I'll come find you and knock some sense into you."

MJ chuckled, and the sound was warm, full of affection. "I wouldn't expect anything less."

Miriam heard Hannah's voice, thick with emotion. "I pray you'll come home someday."

The moment hung between them, tender and raw... too intimate to break. But as soon as their footsteps faded from the hiding spot, Miriam knew what she had to do. She turned and walked swiftly down the length of the barn. MJ's truck was parked just beyond, tucked in the usual spot where his father wouldn't see it. She hesitated only for a moment before pulling the handle. The door clicked open with ease.

Heart hammering in her chest, she climbed inside,

careful not to disturb the neatly packed gear in the backseat. His duffle bag and camping supplies surrounded her, and she spotted an old woolen blanket lying on the floor. Pulling it over herself, she curled up tight, settling between his things, her breath shallow as she listened for any approaching footsteps.

This was it. MJ was leaving, and Miriam was choosing herself for the first time in her life. She wasn't letting him go alone, even if she had to wait in his truck all night.

MIRIAM STIRRED as the truck bounced over a rough patch of road, her body shifting against the duffle bag that had become her makeshift pillow. Disoriented, she blinked into the darkness, the rhythmic hum of the tires on the highway lulling her back to awareness. She had no idea how long they'd been driving, but judging by the dark outside the window and the stiffness in her limbs from being curled up for too long, it had been hours.

A soft tune drifted through the cab, MJ humming low to something on the radio. She took a deep breath, inhaling the scent of dried soybeans and faint traces of barn dust that clung to his things. Her muscles ached, but another discomfort pressed at her, growing more urgent by the second.

She had waited long enough.

Shifting tenderly, she tried to sit up quietly, but the blanket rustled, the sound deafening in the quiet cab. MJ stiffened as he caught her in his rearview mirror. His humming stopped, and a heartbeat later, the truck lurched as he slammed on the brakes, tires skidding on the pavement.

Miriam braced herself as the truck came to a full stop

on the side of the road. For a moment, silence hung thick between them, only the faint tick of the cooling engine breaking it. Then, he turned in his seat, his eyes scanning the back seat, confusion etched on his face.

Miriam swallowed hard. There was no hiding now.

With a sigh, she shoved the blanket aside and sat up, her stiff limbs protesting the movement. "Don't be mad," she muttered before even meeting his gaze.

MJ's mouth fell open. "Miriam?" His voice was low, but there was no missing the disbelief in it. "What—how —" He ran both hands down his face, then shook his head like he couldn't believe what he was seeing. "You've *got* to be kidding me."

She forced an apologetic smile. "Surprise?"

"Surprise?" His voice shot up an octave. "Miriam, what in the name of all that's holy are you doing in my truck?"

She winced. "Riding along?"

"Riding along?" He gestured wildly toward her. "You *snuck* into my truck!"

"Technically, I climbed," she corrected.

"Do you have any idea how insane this is?

Miriam shifted, rubbing the back of her neck. "*Jah.*"

"You've been hiding back there the whole time!"

Miriam cringed. "I dozed off."

MJ's nostrils flared as he muttered something in Pennsylvania Dutch under his breath.

Before he could say another word, she held up a hand. "Look, I swear we can talk about this, but *first…* I need a minute."

MJ frowned. "*A minute?*"

She hesitated, her cheeks warming. "I need to, um… step outside for a moment."

Realization dawned on his face, followed by a look of

exasperation. He scrubbed a hand down his jaw. "Miriam, you've got to be—" He cut himself off with a huff. "Fine. Just hurry up."

Without waiting for his response, she scrambled out of the truck, disappearing behind a stand of trees along the quiet roadside.

MJ groaned, dropping his head against the steering wheel. "Unbelievable," he muttered.

A few minutes later, Miriam climbed back in, this time making herself at home in the front seat and looking noticeably more comfortable. "Okay. Now I'm ready for whatever lecture you have planned."

MJ shook his head, still looking like he might lose his mind. "This is, hands down, the most ridiculous thing you've ever done."

"Maybe," she admitted. "But I had no other choice."

"You had *plenty* of choices. Like staying home, for starters."

Miriam met his gaze, unflinching. "That wasn't an option."

His jaw tensed. "You don't even know where I'm going."

She lifted her chin. "I don't need to."

"This isn't just a little adventure, Miriam. I'm *leaving*. For real. I don't know when, or if I'm coming back."

"I know, and I don't expect you to change your plans because of me."

His fingers flexed on the steering wheel as he studied her. "Then why would you do this?"

Miriam hesitated, then reached into her coat pocket and pulled out a small bundle of folded bills. She held them up between them. "Because I have six hundred dollars and enough sense to know I can pay my own way."

MJ's eyebrows shot up. "You *brought money*?"

She nodded. "*Jah*. And I don't expect you to take care of me. I just need a chance to figure out what I want. Same as you."

MJ gripped the wheel like it was the only thing keeping him grounded. "I'm going to regret this."

Miriam grinned despite the tension. "Probably."

MJ started the truck again, shaking his head as he pulled back onto the road. "First things first, I need coffee. And you—" He shot her a glare. "You're buying."

She smiled. "Deal."

MJ PULLED into the gas station just off the interstate, the neon sign flickering above the pumps as the late morning sun stretched across the asphalt. Miriam stepped out of the truck and followed him into the small convenience store that doubled as a café. The smell of gasoline gave way to the comforting aroma of fresh coffee and bacon sizzling on a griddle behind the counter.

They found a corner booth, shiny, cracked, and a little too exposed for MJ's nerves. He dropped his hat onto the table, rubbed the back of his neck, then slid his fingers to his temples like he could press the conflict out of his skull.

After they placed their order, Miriam sat across from him, fingers wrapped around her mug, steady even as her world tilted off its axis.

MJ stared down at the table. "This isn't how I planned it," he muttered. "You being here... it changes everything."

"I know, but going back isn't an option."

His jaw tightened. "We can't hike together, Miriam. Not just the two of us. You're baptized. You know what kind of trouble that would cause if anyone found out."

"I know the *Ordnung*. But I also know what it's like to be trapped in a life someone else planned for you."

He leaned forward, voice low, fierce. "And you think this is freedom? Sleeping on the ground? No plan, no place to go? I only have one tent. One sleeping bag. We'd have to —" He cut himself off, shaking his head.

She looked down, then back up with quiet strength. "Then I'll sleep under the stars. But I'm not going back. Not yet."

A heavy silence settled between them, broken only by the clatter of silverware behind the counter and the low hum of a refrigeration unit.

Finally, MJ spoke again, his voice softer now, almost afraid. "Do you think this is easy for me? You showing up like this? Miriam…" He paused. "You make me want to be the kind of man who wouldn't let you down. But I don't even know who I am outside of that community."

She met his eyes, searching them. "Do you want me to go?"

His eyes flicked up, locking onto hers.

"*Nee.*" The word slipped out too fast. Too raw. He sat back like it startled even him.

Miriam sucked in a breath slightly, and her voice dropped to a whisper. "Then say that."

"I just did."

For a beat, neither of them looked away.

Something passed between them, unspoken, heavy, trembling with the weight of all they couldn't say. Of all they wanted to say.

Miriam reached again for her coffee, hands barely steady. "You don't have to have it all figured out today. But maybe we could just… start walking. One mile at a time."

MJ ran a hand over his mouth. "I don't know if I can lead you anywhere good."

She gave a small smile. "Then let's just walk side by side and figure it out as we go."

BEFORE EITHER COULD SAY MORE, Miriam stiffened. Her gaze shifted across the cafe, where a familiar face appeared at the register. The *Englisch* woman from the trail, with a kind smile, worn boots, and that same spark of adventure in her eyes, stood paying for her tea.

"It's her," Miriam whispered. "She's from Willow Springs. I met her on the walking trail that winds through our farms."

MJ followed her gaze, heart still thudding. And just like that, the fragile moment between them dissolved, folded up, and tucked away, like a letter never quite mailed.

"You know her?"

"She said she traveled the world."

They both watched in silence as the woman turned, tea in hand, and locked eyes with Miriam. Her smile deepened, as if she recognized something more than just a familiar face.

Maybe the path ahead wasn't so impossible after all, Miriam thought as the woman walked her way.

"Well, well. I thought I recognized those faces." The older woman stood there, her hiking boots dusted from travel, her silver-streaked hair tucked up under a wide-brimmed trail hat. She looked a few decades older than them, but she carried herself like someone half her age with confidence, ease, and a spark of mischief.

Miriam blinked in surprise. "You were on the trail near Willow Springs."

"Sure was." The woman grinned. "Didn't expect to run into you again, but here we are." She turned toward MJ. "And you're the young man from the feed store.

Name's Iona Parker." She stepped forward and extended her hand toward MJ.

MJ stood awkwardly, hesitating a split second before reaching out. Her grip was firm and sure, far different from anything in his world. The handshake felt strange, unfamiliar, and he had no idea what to do with the odd formality of it.

"MJ King." He cleared his throat. "And this is Miriam, but I think you've already met."

Iona nodded, releasing his hand and looking between the two of them with knowing eyes. "You two look like a couple of cats caught in the middle of a road, unsure whether to keep going or run back to the barn."

MJ offered a thin smile. "We're trying to figure a few things out."

"Where are you headed?" Iona asked as she slid into the booth next to Miriam.

MJ hesitated before responding, "I was going to hike the Foothills Trail, but now I'm not too sure." He nodded in Miriam's direction. "She sort of put an unexpected twist in my plans."

"Well, if you're heading to the Foothills Trail, you won't be doing it alone. I've got my gear loaded in the SUV outside and two feet itching to get moving. You'd be surprised how many solo hikers are actually hoping for a little company."

Miriam tilted her head. "You're hiking the trail too?"

"Every mile. And I'd love the company if we're heading in the same direction." Iona winked.

MJ leaned back. "You'd really let us come along?"

"You'd be doing me a favor. Company is good for the soul." Her gaze softened. "And it's clear you two are walking through something deeper than trail plans. I don't know what's weighing you down, but I do know the wilderness has a way of making things plain."

They were both quiet for a moment. Iona sipped from her cup and then casually added, "Besides, this saves you the trouble of explaining yourself." She leaned in and whispered, "I've been around the Amish enough and can only imagine the struggles you're facing."

Miriam let out a soft, surprised laugh. MJ looked down at the table, then back at her.

"I guess it could work," he admitted.

Iona stood. "I'll be gassing up and grabbing a bagel for the road. Meet me at the campground in Oconee State Park; I estimate we'll arrive in about four hours."

With that, she strode toward the front counter, leaving MJ and Miriam to sit in stunned silence.

"Well," MJ murmured, rubbing his jaw, "she's… something."

"She's exactly what we needed."

MJ glanced at Miriam, surprised. She was smiling for the first time that morning.

THE TWO-LANE HIGHWAY unwound through the hills like a slow-moving stream. Budding trees lined the roadside, their pale green leaves shimmering in the breeze. Wildflowers speckled the ditches in shades of yellow, white, and blue. It was as if they were driving straight into another world.

Miriam sat peacefully in the passenger seat, watching the landscape blur past. Every few minutes, she'd catch herself leaning forward a bit, like she didn't want to miss a single thing.

MJ glanced at her and smirked. "You're worse than Hannah when we drive anywhere new."

"I don't think I've ever seen trees like this. It's almost like they're trying to tell you something."

He chuckled. "What would they say?"

She smiled faintly. "That there's more to the world than fences and fields."

The silence returned, but it wasn't uncomfortable. It hung between them like something familiar, like the quiet of a barn before sunrise.

They rode in silence for a stretch, the rhythmic hum of tires filling the space between them. Miriam studied the unfamiliar land, every curve of the hills and sway of the trees like pages from a book she was finally being allowed to read.

After a while, MJ adjusted his grip on the steering wheel and cast her a quick sideways glance and asked, "Why was your mother so set on marrying you off?"

Miriam stiffened ever so slightly, and the corner of her mouth tugged downward.

"She's… worried I won't be able to take care of a family."

MJ's brow furrowed. "Why would she think that?"

After a long pause. Her hands clenched in her lap.

"It's complicated," she whispered as she glanced out the window. "Something I haven't figured out how to talk about. Not yet."

MJ opened his mouth, then closed it again. His grip on the wheel tightened, then loosened. "Alright," he said tenderly. "You don't have to tell me. Not until you're ready."

She looked back at him, something soft and grateful in her expression. "Thank you. For not pressing."

He nodded once. "I'll wait."

They drove on, the quiet between them no longer heavy but tender. In time, the foothills began to rise around them, and the road narrowed into winding curves that promised adventure. Miriam closed her eyes for a moment and whispered a quiet prayer of thanks, for freedom and for the kindness of someone willing to walk beside her, even without all the answers.

Miriam hesitated before turning toward him, her voice more sure now. "I want to see the world. Not all of it. Just some parts of it. Something that doesn't look like Willow Springs. I don't want to wake up one day and realize I missed seeing everything."

He didn't say anything right away. Just tapped his thumb along the wheel and let the tide of her words settle.

"I get that. More than you know."

"Do you think we're being selfish?" she asked after a long moment.

"For leaving?"

She nodded.

He let out a long breath. "Maybe. But maybe staying, knowing you're meant for more, is a different kind of selfish. One that slowly eats you up inside."

She looked at him and offered a small, tired smile. He returned it, with an unspoken understanding she hadn't expected.

Iona's silver SUV was already parked in the designated camping area, and she was crouched beside the fire pit, arranging kindling with the efficiency of someone who had done this a hundred times before.

"About time," she called cheerfully, waving them over with a half-burned branch. "I was starting to think y'all chickened out."

MJ gave a short laugh and stepped out of the truck. "Still time for that."

Miriam climbed down more slowly, shielding her eyes against the lowering sun as it flickered through the trees. The light made it hard to gauge the terrain, and she hesitated until she found her footing.

They got to work unloading gear. Iona's site was already neatly arranged: tent pitched, cookware organized, bear canister ready. She walked them through everything they'd need to survive the next ten days—maps, dehydrated meals, water filtration systems, emergency whistles, and extra layers of clothing for the cold nights. When Miriam glanced around for another tent, Iona shook her head. "No need," she said kindly. "You'll be sharing mine."

Miriam stood near the corner of the picnic table, watching MJ unpack their gear. Her backpack looked so much smaller compared to Iona's equipment, and heat crept into her cheeks... she hadn't come nearly as prepared.

"You alright, dear?" Iona asked, catching Miriam's distant expression.

Miriam forced a smile and nodded. "*Jah.* Just a bit to take in."

"Well, nerves are natural. First-night jitters are part of the package. Wait until you hear an armadillo rustling around your tent at two in the morning. You'll swear it's a bear the size of a wagon."

MJ snorted faintly as he cinched down a tent stake. Miriam tried to laugh, but the knot in her stomach only tightened.

As the last rays of light filtered through the trees, shadows began to shift and dance. Miriam blinked and tried to focus, but the forest began to blur at the edges. The contrast between light and dark made it harder to judge distance, and every shape seemed to bend into something else. A simple stump became a crouching figure; a pile of leaves shimmered like it might move.

She sat down on the picnic bench, gripping the wood to steady herself. The warmth from the sun had faded abruptly, and so had her confidence. What had she been thinking? Out here, there would be no porch light, no familiar trail, no safe horizon to fix her eyes on. Only darkness. Only unknown. Miriam stared into the flames, the flickering light giving some comfort. But the ache of doubt was hard to shake.

She couldn't tell them, not yet. How could she explain the panic that crept in when shadows swallowed the night from her sight?

She said nothing. Just watched the fire grow, and held tightly to the quiet promise she'd made to herself: to see what she could, while she still could.

CHAPTER 11

*E*velyn's voice rose up the stairs like clockwork, sharp and sure as the morning sun slipped through the kitchen window. She waited a beat, arms crossed, then called again, louder this time.

"Miriam! Time to get up!"

Silence.

With a huff, she climbed the stairs, muttering under her breath about laziness and disrespect. She rapped twice on the bedroom door before pushing it open.

The bed was neatly made.

The room, still and far too tidy, was wrong in a way Evelyn couldn't explain. Her eyes darted from the window to the empty pegs near the door. The small, familiar backpack was gone from the corner of the room.

Her breath caught, and she sucked in a loud sigh. She turned on her heel and stormed out the front door, shielding her eyes from the sun as she spotted Bennie across the yard, already elbow-deep in the morning chores.

"She's gone," she announced, briskly making her way toward him.

Bennie looked up from the feed bucket, his brow furrowed. "What do you mean—gone?"

"She's not in her room. Bed's made, bag's gone. I'm sure she snuck out early and headed to Hannah's before we were even awake." Evelyn waved it off like it was obvious. "I'm going to go get her."

Bennie turned to face her. "Give her a little space. She's probably still sore after the other night."

Guilt teetered on Evelyn's conscience as she remembered the look of disgust on Miriam's face when she caught her burning her books and letters, but she couldn't breathe a word to Bennie about what she'd done.

"One little disagreement," she snapped, "and this is the thanks I get? I was trying to help her see reason."

Bennie snarled, "Helping her see reason or pushing her into a corner?"

Evelyn bristled. "She's young and foolish. Someone has to be the voice of sense."

"And maybe that someone pushed too hard."

Evelyn turned and strode toward the buggy without another word.

When Evelyn pulled up to the King farm, and Hannah answered the door, Evelyn didn't even bother with a greeting.

"Where is she?"

Hannah blinked, confused. "Who?"

"Miriam. Don't play games. I know she came here."

Hannah stepped outside, pulling the door closed behind her. "Evelyn, I haven't seen Miriam since, well, since Sunday. Is something wrong?"

The older woman's lips parted somewhat, but no words came. The color drained from her face.

"You mean… she's not with you?"

"*Nee.*" Hannah's voice grew serious.

Evelyn took a shaky step back, the fight draining from her shoulders. "She's not home. She's not anywhere."

Only then did the grip of it settle, the sharp ache of fear cutting through the pride she'd been holding onto so tightly.

And for the first time, Evelyn Troyer wondered if she had completely pushed her daughter too far.

HANNAH STOOD ON THE PORCH, her arms crossed tightly over her chest as Evelyn climbed back into the buggy, her lips pursed with frustration. The older woman gave a quick, sharp flick of the reins, and the horse trotted down the lane without so much as a thank you or goodbye.

Hannah watched until the buggy disappeared down the road, the clip-clop of hooves fading into the warm hush of the morning. Then she took a deep breath and stepped down into the yard, letting her eyes drift toward the barn.

Her heart sank. *You don't think…*

She'd thought of it before, of course. Last night, MJ had told her he was leaving, that he couldn't stay trapped in a life that wasn't his. That he didn't belong.

And he'd mentioned Miriam.

"She's better off without me."

But even then, Hannah had caught something in his voice. Regret. Longing. Something unspoken.

What if Miriam had been there?

What if she had heard everything?

134

Hannah's eyes drifted toward the back lane, the one MJ used to hide his truck. It had been gone this morning, earlier than usual. At the time, she'd assumed he was trying to avoid *Datt's* wrath. But now…

A chill moved through her despite the sun warming the hem of her dress. She didn't have proof. But she had a sister's instinct. *They're together.* Somewhere out there, Miriam, stubborn and quiet and brave in her own way, and MJ, restless and wild-hearted, were on the road trying to escape all that tried to decide their futures.

Hannah pressed her fingers to her lips, staring out toward the open fields. Part of her wanted to run to her parents, to say something, to sound the alarm. But if they had left together, maybe they weren't just running away. Perhaps they were ultimately running toward something so much bigger.

THE SUN WAS JUST REACHING the tops of the trees when they pulled into the gravel parking area near the trailhead at Oconee State Park. A light morning mist curled along the edges of the path's opening, and dew clung to the leaves of the mountain laurel.

Iona parked her SUV and stepped out, her energy that of someone half her age, already tying her bandana around her neck and reaching for the rear hatch. MJ was right behind her, stretching his arms over his head as if trying to shake off the weight of the last few days.

Miriam lingered for a moment before sliding out of the back seat, her fingers brushing the fabric of her backpack. Inside were her essentials, some snacks, and the rolled-up sleeping pad MJ had insisted she take. The walking poles stood propped beside her, ready for the trail.

MJ had driven his truck to the end of their planned route at Table Rock State Park the day before. Iona had followed behind, stopping at the only hiking supply store near the trailhead before returning to their campsite.

The night had been filled with careful organization, with gear laid out like puzzle pieces across the pine needles. Between MJ's surplus and Iona's well-worn supplies and her new supplies, they'd made sure she had all she needed to pull her own weight for the adventure ahead.

Iona clapped her hands together and grinned at them over the open tailgate. "Alright, you two," her eyes sparkled. "This first stretch is one of my favorites. We'll follow the white blazes, little rectangles painted on trees, about eye level. Can't miss them. We'll pass waterfalls, creeks, and some lovely flat stretches before the hills come in."

She handed Miriam a laminated map and pointed. "This leg is mostly gentle. Good way to warm up your trail legs."

MJ nodded, scanning the tree line as if already envisioning the hike ahead.

Before they shouldered their packs, Iona paused. "Mind if we pray before we get started?"

Miriam glanced at MJ, then back at Iona. She hesitated, but only for a breath before giving a small nod.

Iona stepped close and bowed her head, one hand resting lightly on her trekking pole. "*Lord, thank You for this trail, for the air in our lungs and the strength in our legs. Thank You for new paths and for old wounds that are healing. Walk before us, beside us, and behind us. Give us grace for each step and wonder for what we'll see. And let us never forget Who made all this beauty. Amen.*"

Miriam never heard someone pray like that, not in public, not out loud, not with so much… warmth. In her community, prayer was sacred, yes, but private. Quiet. Reserved. This prayer felt like a conversation with a friend. Something inside her stirred, and she wanted to hear more to understand the depth of Iona's faith.

They set off, their boots crunching the soft dirt, poles tapping in rhythm with their steps. Miriam caught the first white blaze a few trees in—a simple painted rectangle—and smiled.

MJ KEPT a steady pace behind Miriam, watching as the hem of her long skirt flicked in time with her stride. Iona was a few dozen yards ahead, moving like she'd been born on a trail. Miriam moved more slowly, more carefully, her hiking poles digging deep with each step.

He told himself it was because she wasn't used to trails like this, not with the slight incline and the occasional root sticking out like a tripwire. He told himself it was practical for him to follow her, just in case she needed help. But it wasn't just that.

There was something different about her that morning. A heavy, worrisome look covered her face, and it concerned him. Her hair began to loosen in the back, and a few wisps clung to the rim of her *kapp*. She hadn't said much since they started, just a quiet "ready" before they set off and a soft "*denki*" when he adjusted the strap on her pack before they left the parking lot.

And now, as she paused to take a sip from her water bottle, he noticed the slightest tremble in her hand. She was struggling.

Not enough to stop, not enough to admit it, but enough that it pulled something tight inside him. She was breathing harder now. Her steps weren't quite as steady as they'd been earlier. Her walking poles dug deeper into the earth, like she needed them more than she was letting on.

He quickened his pace to walk beside her. "You okay?"

She didn't look at him right away. "*Jah*. Just… adjusting."

"To what?"

"To everything."

He could have asked more. Should have. But something in her voice warned him off. So, instead, he nodded and fell back into place behind her.

As they started up a gentle rise, he saw it again, the slight catch in her step, as if her feet were unsure of what the ground was doing beneath her. She stumbled, not badly, but enough to make his heart lurch. Her pole caught her just in time.

"Careful," he stepped closer.

"I've got it," she replied, breathless but firm.

He wanted to press her. Ask why she was pushing so hard, what she wasn't telling him, why she looked over her shoulder more often than someone who was just admiring the view. But he didn't. Not yet.

Instead, he watched her walk; watched the way she squared her shoulders, even when she was clearly tired. Watched the way her eyes flicked across the trail, cautious, almost like she couldn't quite trust what she was seeing.

And then it hit him. She wasn't just being careful. She was struggling to see what was on the ground in front of her.

A cold ripple passed through him. He quickened his steps to be closer in case she stumbled again. "I'll follow behind you. I'm right behind you in case you need anything."

Miriam didn't respond right away, but then she glanced over her shoulder and gave the smallest nod.

THE TRAIL NARROWED beneath Miriam's boots, winding deeper into the woods. She kept her eyes trained on the path under her feet, but the constant flicker of sunlight and shadow made it hard to see what was ahead. Dappled patches of light stung her vision, then disappeared again, swallowed by the dense green of the forest. It was more disorienting than she'd expected.

She adjusted her grip on her poles, feeling the sweat on her palms. Light bent and broke through the leaves in unpredictable ways, and the confidence she'd been clinging to started to crack.

The further they walked, the more she realized how much she had underestimated the shadows. They were everywhere, blurring her depth perception, turning harmless stones into threats and small roots into danger. Every time she blinked, the world shifted again. Her throat tightened. Maybe this had been a mistake.

She had wanted to believe she could do this, that she could see just enough, hear just enough, trust just enough. But now the fear had curled up inside her, pressing heavy against her chest.

She didn't want to slow them down. She didn't want MJ to look at her with pity or Iona to regret taking her along. She had told herself she wasn't a burden, but what if she was wrong?

Miriam bit the inside of her cheek and took a slow, careful step forward. Breathe. Listen. If she couldn't trust her eyes, then she'd trust what was left.

The sound of MJ's steady footfalls behind her gave her comfort. She knew he was there, even if he said nothing. She needed to steady herself. To silence the panic.

Without thinking, she started to hum. Just a soft tune at

first, almost under her breath. A song from her childhood... the one she always returned to when the world grew too big or too dark.

Amazing grace, how sweet the sound...

The words rose slowly from her lips, steadying her feet. As if the rhythm of the hymn guided her one step at a time. *...that saved a wretch like me...*

Her voice was quiet, and after a few verses, she heard something surprising... MJ's low voice joined in from behind, barely more than a whisper.

Then, Iona, ahead of them, took it up too, her voice richer, full of something like joy, or a memory she was reliving.

Their voices blended together, and for a few sacred moments, fear and uncertainty slipped away. She didn't think about what she couldn't see or what she might lose in the years ahead. Only peace remained. As the final verse fell from their lips, she whispered it like a prayer: *was blind, but now I see.*

She smiled faintly as the silence returned to the forest. She didn't know how she would make it to the end of this journey.

But at that moment, she knew she didn't have to do it alone.

THEY MADE camp that first night without much talking. Fatigue settled deep in Miriam's bones, heavier than she expected. Her legs were stiff, her shoulders sore, and her eyes heavy from a day spent navigating dancing light and shifting shadows. But even so, a quiet thankfulness stirred within her.

She sat on a flat rock near the fire pit, her hiking boots

off and her sweater wrapped over her shoulders. The fire crackled to life, and warmth began to spread through their small circle.

Iona sat, legs crossed beneath her, her silver-streaked hair pulled back in a thick braid. "You did good today, Miriam. The first day's always the hardest."

Miriam managed a small smile. "I didn't expect it to be so... overwhelming. But thank you. For everything."

MJ leaned back on his hands, stretching out his long legs toward the fire as he watched the flames flicker. "You didn't complain once."

"I wanted to," Miriam murmured with a wry grin.

Iona chuckled. "Honesty. Good. You'll need that out here." She poked at the fire with a stick, the flames glowing on her weathered face. "You know, the first trail I ever hiked alone was a mess. I packed too much, got blisters the size of walnuts, and cried half the first night because the stars looked so strange without my husband next to me."

Miriam blinked. She hadn't expected that.

"How long were you married?" MJ asked.

"Forty years." Iona's voice softened with memory. "My Bill was a preacher. Big-hearted. Always full of words." She smiled to herself. "He dragged me all over the world doing missions, speaking, supporting churches in tiny corners of the globe. I thought I'd never know peace standing still."

She paused, watching a spark drift skyward.

"When he passed... it was like the map we'd drawn together suddenly disappeared. For months, I didn't know who I was without him. I tried to be the version of me people expected: quiet, grieving, grateful for a good life." She met Miriam's eyes. "But I didn't feel alive."

Miriam listened, the rhythm of the falls behind them echoing Iona's words.

"And then I found the trails. Nature doesn't ask anything of you except that you show up and keep going. And somewhere in the silence of the woods, with the trees creaking overhead and the dirt under my boots, I realized I still had life in me. And not just life, but *purpose*. A story to write that wasn't finished just because someone else's was."

Miriam looked down at her hands, thinking of all the stories she thought had already been written for her.

"I suppose that's why I hike now. To remember I still have steps to take. That this earth, and the beauty God filled it with, isn't wasted when we walk through it with eyes open. Even when those eyes can't always see as clearly as they once did."

Miriam's breath caught. Her face flushed, but Iona wasn't watching her, she was staring into the fire, as if the memory of her husband still warmed her from the inside.

MJ sat silently beside them, the firelight flickering across his profile. Miriam didn't dare look at him. She wasn't sure she could, not with the secret she'd been keeping from them still simmering to be released.

She hadn't told them everything. Not yet. But maybe… just maybe, this was the path that would help her find the courage to do so, and hopefully, it would help her face her fears of the future along the way.

CHAPTER 12

*T*he forest outside the tent lay quiet when Miriam's eyes fluttered open. A dull ache pulsed in her lower abdomen, and she knew she couldn't wait any longer. The early morning chill crept in around the edges of her sleeping bag, and she slid out, trying not to wake Iona. The older woman breathed softly, undisturbed beneath their shared tent canvas.

Miriam unzipped the tent quietly and stepped out into the cool of pre-dawn. The fire pit still smoldered faintly nearby as she pulled her sweater tighter around her, stepped into her hiking boots, and was thankful she had thought to slip on her leggings before bed.

She remembered the tree she'd seen before sunset, not far from camp, a large hemlock with low-hanging branches that provided privacy. Clutching her flashlight, she made her way carefully, keeping her steps light.

But as she stepped over a root, her foot caught, and she stumbled. Her flashlight flew from her hand and hit the ground with a muted thud. The beam flickered, sputtered, and then went dark.

"*Nee...*" she whispered, kneeling to feel blindly along the forest floor. Her fingers brushed damp leaves, twigs, and moss, but no flashlight.

Panic settled in her chest. She turned instinctively to head back toward camp, but everything looked the same. Every direction seemed shadowed and unfamiliar. The faint smoldering light from the fire was lost behind a wall of trees. She stopped and took a moment to clean her glasses, hoping to make her view clearer before moving further in the direction she thought she had gone.

Determined not to panic, she kept walking, her hands stretched out in front of her, trying to feel her way through the dense dark. But as she stepped onto what she thought was solid ground, the earth beneath her gave way. With a startled cry, she slid down a muddy embankment, branches scraping her arms as she fell. Her glasses flew from her face and disappeared into the dark. She landed hard at the bottom of a shallow ravine, breath knocked from her lungs.

Pain radiated through her side, and her dress and leggings were soaked through with cold mud. She sat for a moment, stunned, trying to make sense of what had just happened. Her heart pounded against her ribs.

The realization hit her hard. She couldn't see well enough to find her way back. Not in this darkness. Not without help. Her mother's words echoed in her mind, words laced with doubt and fear. Maybe she wasn't capable of managing on her own.

Tears welled in her eyes, but she instantly blinked them away. Crying wouldn't help. Still, a fresh wave of helplessness swept over her as she stood and tried to climb back up the muddy slope, only to slip and fall again.

Exhausted, shivering, and disoriented, she crawled

toward a tree and leaned against it. Her whole body trembled, and her wet clothes clung to her skin.

Her breathing quickened. Then she remembered something she'd read in one of the hiking books MJ had brought her. *If you get turned around, don't wander. Stop. Sit. Let someone find you.*

Heart pounding, she lowered herself to the base of a nearby tree and curled up tightly. She drew her dress over her bent knees and pressed herself against the bark. Her sweater provided some warmth, but the damp forest air gnawed at her cheeks and fingers.

Still, it wasn't the cold that gripped her. It was the dark. The shadows were thick, unrelenting, pressing in at all sides. Shapes twisted in her central vision, and even when she closed her eyes, they danced behind her lids. It was the kind of darkness she hated most, the kind she couldn't fight.

She clung to her other senses. The rustle of small animals in the brush. The occasional hoot of an owl. The creak of trees shifting faintly in the wind. None of it was frightening, not like the dark.

It reminded her of what was coming. Of what the doctors hinted might one day be permanent, of what her mother always whispered behind closed doors.

She might never see her way out again. Tears welled and fell freely this time. "What will I do if it really happens? If this isn't just a moment, but my whole life?" she whispered to the night.

She bowed her head and folded her hands, whispering, *"Please, Lord. I need You. I can't do this alone. Guide MJ and Iona. Bring them to me. Maybe this is how You'll lead me,"* she prayed quietly. *"Maybe You'll give me new ways to see. But I'm scared, Lord. Terrified. I don't want to be a burden. Not to MJ. Not to anyone."*

But somewhere beyond the trees, she believed MJ was already searching. She only had to wait. And trust.

THE LIGHT HAD BARELY STARTED to seep through the tent when Iona stirred and sat up. She blinked against the dull gray light, stretching her back and rubbing her eyes. The air was brisk, but not biting, and the familiar scent of damp earth filled her lungs.

She turned toward Miriam's side of the tent. Empty.

Frowning, she unzipped the flap and stepped outside, scanning the edge of camp. "Miriam?" she called, "you out here?"

Only the whisper of wind and the rustle of trees answered back. MJ emerged from his tent a few minutes later, tugging on his boots. "Something wrong?"

"She's not here. I figured she went off to find a tree, but... she's not answering."

A line formed between MJ's brows. He glanced around quickly, then strode toward the tree line. "Miriam!" he called.

Nothing.

They waited, pacing the edges of camp, calling every few minutes. Ten minutes passed. Then fifteen.

"I shouldn't have brought her," MJ muttered, running a hand through his hair. "I knew this was a mistake. She's not built for this, physically or... or emotionally. I should've put my foot down."

Iona turned sharply, her eyes flashing with a quiet intensity. "Don't say that."

"She's not ready! I knew it, and I still let her come. I just—" He blew out a breath and looked toward the trees.

"I thought I could look out for her. I should've stayed closer. I should've checked…"

"She's not a child," Iona interrupted. "She's out here for a reason. She's carrying something heavy, I don't know what, but I've been around long enough to know when someone's fighting to prove something to themselves."

MJ's jaw clenched. "She's probably scared out of her mind right now. And it's my fault."

Iona stepped forward and placed a firm hand on his shoulder. "Hiking has a way of bringing out things buried deep inside us. Fear. Strength. Faith. You think she's not capable of this, but I've seen something else in her… *determination.*"

He looked away, the muscles in his jaw working.

"She needs this," Iona continued. "Maybe more than either of us understands. But right now, she needs to be found. You head north toward the creek. I'll take the path to the east. Blow your whistle if you find her."

MJ gave a tense nod, then turned and took off through the underbrush, his boots pounding soft earth and fallen leaves.

As Iona moved into the trees in the opposite direction, she whispered a silent prayer of her own. *Help us find her, Lord. And help her find herself.*

MIRIAM DOZED ON AND OFF, unsure how much time had passed. The ache in her side hadn't dulled, but the fear had begun to fade with the morning light.

As the first pale light crept into the sky, she opened her eyes. The woods were still cloaked in blue shadow, but the crushing darkness had lifted. Miriam looked up the muddy slope. The incline looked twice as steep in the weak morning light.

She pushed herself upright and took a cautious step toward it. Her boots sank somewhat in the soft earth. She placed her hands against the slope, clawing for purchase. Halfway up, she slipped and tumbled back to the bottom, the impact jarring her already sore side.

Tears stung her eyes, but she bit them back.

She took a breath, then another. "Fear is not from You," she whispered. "Peace is."

It was something she'd read, something that had burrowed deep in her heart. Fear was from the enemy. Peace came from *Gott*. She repeated the truth silently as she tried again.

MJ's EYES landed on something just past camp. A flashlight. Mud-smeared and half-buried in the leaves. He sprinted toward it, snatching it up. The casing was cracked, and when he pressed the button, it flickered weakly and died. He looked around. The ground was soft from last night's rain, and faint impressions marred the surface, just enough for him to make out the shape of boots. Hers.

MJ didn't wait. He plunged into the trees, following the faintest hints of her presence: a flattened brush, bent ferns, a single torn thread of her dress clinging to a branch. The morning light filtered through the canopy, adding streaks across the forest floor, but it did little to ease the tight knot in his chest.

He should've never let her come. What had he been thinking? She wasn't ready for this kind of trail, this kind of danger. He'd been so focused on getting away from his own problems, his father, the farm, the life that had closed in around him like a cage, that he hadn't seen hers.

Until now, each step forward had grown heavier, as if he were dragging a revelation with him. He wasn't scared because she was lost; he was terrified because he couldn't imagine her gone. The truth struck hard, like a blow to the chest... *he cared for her.*

The realization stole his breath. He wasn't even sure when it had happened. Somewhere between their quiet letters and the way she nibbled on her lip when she was lost in thought. Somewhere in her laugh, her stubbornness, the way she faced the world, even when it had given her every reason to turn away.

And now... she was out here. Alone. Cold. Maybe hurt.

He pressed a hand to his chest, trying to steady himself. *"Please, Gott,"* he whispered. *"Lead me to her."*

The forest seemed to quiet as he pushed forward, each footprint he spotted driving him faster through the underbrush. He no longer cared about the mud soaking into his boots or the sting of branches snapping against his face.

All that mattered was Miriam. He had to find her.

Miriam slid back down to her hidden spot at the bottom of the dark ravine. She tried again... this time, she used her whole body, hands grasping at roots and brambles, boots digging into the earth. She sang softly as she climbed, the words of *Amazing Grace* trembling off her lips.

"Amazing grace... how sweet the sound..."

Her voice wavered but didn't stop. Each verse steadied her. Each step pushed her higher. At long last, breathless and muddy, she reached the top. She paused at the edge, gripping a low branch to steady herself. Her heart thundered, her fingers throbbed, but she had done it.

∼

MJ BROKE through the thicket just as the ridge leveled out, and there she was. Crumpled at the rim of the slope, her dress muddied, her body curled inward, perfectly still.

His breath caught in his throat. "Miriam!" he called, rushing forward, all else forgotten.

She stirred slightly as he dropped to his knees beside her. Relief flooded him, swift and sharp. "I'm here." He tried to steady the tremor in his voice.

Her eyes opened, slow and heavy, as she gave him a faint smile. "You found me."

He reached out instinctively, brushing the dirt from her cheek, but when his fingers met her skin… cold, damp, far too pale, he paused. The contact startled him more than it should have. He pulled his hand back abruptly, curling it into a fist against his thigh.

Still, he needed to be sure she was all right.

"Are you hurt?" he asked, scanning her quickly.

"I slipped and lost my glasses," she muttered, her voice weak but clear. "My side aches, but I don't think anything's broken."

He hesitated, then lightly ran his hands down her arms and legs, checking for swelling or injury, all the while avoiding her eyes. When he finished, he sat back on his heels, visibly shaken but trying to compose himself.

"You're lucky," he muttered, more to himself than to her. "You could've broken something out here. Could've—"

He stopped mid-sentence, fumbling for the emergency

whistle hanging around his neck. The sharp sound pierced the still night air, echoing through the trees … a signal to Iona that he'd found Miriam. For a long moment, only silence answered. Then the faint crunch of footsteps above told him Iona was on her way.

He stopped. Swallowed.

She looked at him tenderly. "But I didn't."

He stood and extended a hand to her without a word. She took it. The moment their palms touched, something passed between them. Once she was on her feet, he let go promptly and stepped aside, brushing his hands off on his pants.

The sun was beginning to rise through the thinning canopy above them. He nodded toward the trail. "Let's get you back, but let me see if I can find your glasses."

She reached for his arm, her breath still shallow but steady. "Don't bother, I have another pair in my bag."

As they walked side by side, MJ kept a half-step behind her, watching her closer now, noticing things he hadn't before. Something had changed in him. The fear he'd felt when she was gone had carved a space inside him that wouldn't close.

THEY RETURNED to camp in silence. MJ immediately set to work rebuilding the fire. The flick of his lighter and the crackling of twigs helped push back the remaining chill.

Miriam sank onto a log near the flames, wrapping her sleeping bag around her shoulders. Mud streaked her dress and leggings, and her *kapp* was muddy and damp, but she didn't complain. Her hands hovered near the fire, soaking in the warmth.

Iona emerged from the trail minutes later, relief

washing over her face when she saw Miriam safe. Miriam glanced up at them both. "I'm sorry, I didn't mean to scare you."

MJ didn't answer right away. He stared into the fire, his jaw tight.

"I shouldn't have come," she whispered.

MJ looked at her then, eyes filled with conflict. "You scared the life out of me. You could've been seriously hurt, or worse."

"But I wasn't." She took a breath. "Please, just let me finish the hike. Let me see it through. And after that, you can take me home. I'll go without a fuss."

They sat in silence for a moment, watching the flames dance. The tension eased a touch, replaced by something quieter. Respect. Understanding. Maybe even something deeper, waiting just under the surface.

MIRIAM SAT CLOSE to the fire, her damp leggings steaming slightly in the rising warmth. Iona and MJ busied themselves behind her, packing their gear with solemn efficiency. The events of the morning had sobered them all. As Miriam watched the flames curl and crackle, the heaviness of unspoken truth pressed down on her.

She pulled her knees up under her dress and rested her chin on them, debating. The moment was too quiet, too sacred to speak her truth aloud. But it was time. She couldn't keep this to herself any longer.

She took a slow breath and turned a tad so her voice would carry. "I need to tell you both something."

MJ and Iona paused what they were doing. Iona stepped closer and lowered herself onto a nearby log, and MJ crouched just behind her.

"It's about my eyes," Miriam began. "I haven't been completely honest. I—I have a rare genetic condition. My central vision is deteriorating. Over time, it will get worse... I won't go totally blind. My peripheral vision will stay, but the middle, the part I need to read, to sew, to do any fine detail, it's already blurry most of the time."

MJ opened his mouth, but said nothing at first. His eyes, usually sharp with thought, now seemed soft and wounded, as if the news hit him unexpectedly. "Miriam," he whispered, "why didn't you tell me?"

"I didn't want you to look at me differently, and I didn't want pity. Or protection. I just wanted to feel capable. Normal."

MJ opened his mouth, then closed it again. He stared into the fire like it might give him the right words. "I wouldn't have looked at you differently, but I might've tried to talk you out of coming."

Miriam offered a weak smile. "Exactly. That's why I got lost," she continued. "It's especially hard in dim light or shadows. I couldn't tell which direction was which. Everything blurs together, and the more I panic, the worse it gets. I didn't want to be a burden," Miriam whispered.

A silence settled in, not heavy, just full. Then Iona stepped in, brushing her hands off on her hiking pants and sitting on a nearby log, her face calm and steady.

"You know... when my husband got sick—real sick— we started saying things like 'This is too much,' 'We're not going to make it,' 'What if God doesn't come through?' Little phrases that slip in when things get hard."

She looked at Miriam and then MJ. "One day, he stopped me mid-sentence and said, 'Honey, we can't speak death over what God has already promised to redeem.' That stuck with me."

She poked the fire with a stick, sparks floating up into

the air. "There's power in our words," she continued. "Proverbs says it plain… life and death are in the tongue. When we speak defeat, we start to live like we've already lost. But when we speak hope, even just a sliver of it, we leave space for God to work."

Miriam swallowed. "My *mamm*… she's been saying all the worst things, like how I won't be able to care for a family. That I'll need someone to look after me." Miriam stopped and took a deep breath before continuing. "She means well, but… it's all fear. And it's gotten into me. I hear her voice even when she's not around."

Iona leaned forward, her eyes kind and fierce all at once. "Then it's time to replace her voice with truth. You don't belong to fear, Miriam. And you don't owe your future to anyone's dread. You speak life over your eyes, over your path, over what God still has for you. You say thank you for what you *can* do instead of grieving what might never happen."

She gave a firm nod. "That's how you break those word curses… by speaking blessings in their place."

MJ looked between the two women, his jaw clenched slightly. "I should've known something was wrong. I should've protected you."

"*Nee*, you've given me the freedom to try. That's what I needed."

Iona squeezed her hand. "This hike? This whole journey? It's not about proving your worth. It's about remembering who gave it to you in the first place."

Miriam smiled, tears glittering in her lashes. "Thank you."

"No more apologies, from either of you. We're going to finish this hike together. And we're going to speak life every step of the way."

MJ gave a quiet huff of laughter. "Even when it rains?"

"Especially when it rains." Iona grinned. "That's when we learn to dance in the mud."

They all laughed, the fire popping cheerfully between them. And for the first time in a long while, a bit of lightness returned to Miriam... not because her burden had vanished, but because she wasn't carrying it alone.

CHAPTER 13

The forest held a stillness, quiet and reverent, as the trio followed a narrow bend in the trail. Iona walked ahead, her hiking poles tapping a steady rhythm against the rocky soil. MJ stayed in the rear, his eyes often lifting to check on Miriam, who stayed a few steps ahead, focused and quiet.

They were well past the halfway point of the Foothills Trail, with two long days behind them since Bear Creek and the last major rest stop before their final climb to Table Rock. Spirits had been high that morning until they hit the detour.

A recent washout from an early spring storm had taken out a wooden footbridge that once crossed a shallow ravine. A sign marked the way with an arrow and the words "ALTERNATE ROUTE" tacked to the aged sign.

"Well." Iona planted her poles and squinted at the worn map MJ unfolded. "Looks like we'll be adding some mileage today. Could be three, maybe four extra miles."

Miriam, who'd come up beside her, stared into the stretch of woods where the detour led. It looked less maintained, narrower, more overgrown. "We'll have enough daylight to get to the next site?"

"If we keep a steady pace and don't lollygag, we'll be fine. But it'll be a long one. You two up for that?"

MJ looked at Miriam. She gave a single, sure nod.

By MIDAFTERNOON, the detour had taken its toll. The sun dipped behind a thicket of pines, and the path was steep in places, weaving around boulders and slipping into valleys where the air grew damper and the temperature cooler. The trail markings were fewer, and at times, the trio had to backtrack to stay on course.

"You know," MJ grumbled as they paused for water, "this is starting to feel personal. Like the trail's trying to teach us something."

Iona laughed. "That's exactly what it's doing."

Miriam didn't laugh. She was quiet, her face pale, her steps growing slower.

"You okay?" MJ asked as they resumed walking, catching up to walk beside her.

"It's just a lot of light and shadow. Makes it hard to see where the ground dips. I'm fine."

He frowned. "Let me take your pack. Just for a little bit."

"I said I'm fine," she said, more sharply than she meant to.

He didn't argue, just kept pace.

They continued in silence for another hour. Then, as the trail curved around a narrow slope, Miriam slipped. She fell forward with a gasp, catching herself on her hands.

"Miriam!" MJ dropped beside her.

"I'm okay, just… embarrassed."

"Nothing to be embarrassed about." He offered a hand, but she pushed herself up without it.

Iona had turned around by then, concern in her eyes. "Let's take a break. There's a clearing up ahead."

The clearing wasn't much, just a patch of mossy ground with a few big boulders to rest on. But to Miriam, it was the most welcome place in the world. She dropped her pack and sat cross-legged, breathing deeply, letting the tension leak from her shoulders.

They sat in silence for a while. Miriam stared at her hands, the faint scrape on her palm from her fall. She flexed her fingers. "Back home," she muttered, "I always thought I had to prove I could do things to my mother, to everyone. But I think... maybe I really needed to prove it to myself."

"And?" MJ asked.

She smiled. "I'm getting there."

Iona stretched her legs out. "Well, I've found that when we think we're lost or off course, that's usually when God shows us something important. Sometimes, the detour is the destination."

MJ arched a brow. "Is that one of your husband's old sayings again?"

"Nope." She smiled as she strapped on her pack. "That one's all mine."

MJ sat beside Miriam, their shoulders nearly touching.

"That section was hard."

"Yeah," he agreed. "But it was a good hard, *jah*?"

She looked at him, and for once, he didn't look away.

"*Denki*."

"For what?"

"Letting me fall and letting me get back up on my own."

He just smiled.

~

Miriam had seen a sliver of open space between two hemlocks and told MJ she was going to wander a few hundred yards back to the spot she had noticed along the trail. "I want to sit by the creek for a little while. I brought my notebook."

MJ nodded a little reluctantly and watched her until she slipped between the trees.

Now, with her journal tucked under one arm and the sun warming her back, Miriam slowed her steps, letting her ears guide her. The trail had curved gently away from the creek, but she could still hear its steady whisper somewhere nearby. Then came a gentle, rhythmic splash. She paused, tilting her head. A soft croak. Then, another flutter of wings and the sharp, clean call of a blue heron. A smile touched her lips. Water. She was close.

She followed the sound carefully, one foot after the other, adjusting for the way the light played tricks on her eyes in the shadows. The shimmering movement of water between trees grew clearer, brighter. Finally, she stepped into a small clearing with a flat rock resting at the edge of the stream. The sun struck the surface just so, making the whole scene glow. She breathed it in like a prayer.

Sitting down, Miriam opened her journal and ran her fingers over the first blank page. She let the quiet settle before she began to write.

Dear Lord,

I don't know why You chose to walk me down this particular path, but today, I want to thank You. Thank You for the steady rhythm of the water. Thank You for the breeze that helped me find my way. Thank You for my ears, for the way You've made other things louder and clearer when my eyes fall short. You knew what I'd need before I even asked.

I used to think losing part of my sight would be the end of everything I knew. I was afraid of needing help, of being a burden, of being seen as less-than. But these days out here have taught me something else. They've taught me that maybe my strength doesn't come from seeing everything clearly. But from trusting You.

MJ has been so patient with me. I don't know what I would have done if he hadn't said yes to letting me come. He watches out for me without making me feel broken. I can feel his care in the small things, the way he slows his steps when the shadows get long, the way he checks our footing, even when he pretends it's for himself.

And Lord, I don't want this to be the last time we walk side by side. I know I shouldn't ask for more than You've already given. But if there is room in Your plan… if MJ is meant to find his way home, not just to Willow Springs but to You… then let that be so.

Not for me. Not just because I care for him. But because I see in him something good and kind and loyal, something that reminds me of You.

I don't know what comes next. But for today, I am thankful.

Miriam

Miriam closed her journal slowly and held it in her lap, pressing her palm flat against the cover. Her eyes drifted closed as the warmth of the sun soaked into her shoulders, and for the first time since their hike began, she didn't feel like she was running to prove something. She just felt... steady.

After a few more moments, she stood slowly, brushing the dirt from her skirt and tucking the journal under her arm again. The sound of the creek guided her back to the main trail and back to MJ and Iona.

THE TRAIL NARROWED AGAIN, curling around a thicket of rhododendrons and angling upward into a rocky incline that hadn't looked half as steep on the map. MJ shifted the weight of his pack higher on his shoulders and took the next step. His left foot landed wrong, just enough to feel the twist and pain jabbed up his ankle like a bee sting. He winced and froze mid-step.

"*Goot* grief," he muttered, shifting his weight back and flexing his ankle.

Miriam turned and headed back his way, her poles tapping against the dirt in a steady rhythm. "Everything alright?"

"*Jah*, just… missed my footing. I'm fine."

She didn't look convinced. "You're limping on it."

"It's nothing."

"You sure?"

"I said I'm fine." MJ sighed and reached for a tree to balance himself. "Sorry. I didn't mean to snap."

She stepped closer, glancing down at his boot. "Can you walk?"

He tested it again. "Hurts some. Not bad. Just rolled it."

"Sit down for a few minutes before you make it worse."

He started to argue but caught himself. Instead, he eased onto a low boulder and unlaced his boot. She crouched down, balancing her weight on one pole, and took out the small first aid kit Iona had insisted they carry. He watched her work, calm, quiet, deliberate, as she wrapped his ankle.

"You've been taking care of me. But that doesn't mean you have to carry the weight all by yourself. I can take care of you too."

He swallowed hard, throat tight. "I'm not used to needing anyone."

She smiled faintly. "Neither am I."

"I never noticed how strong you are."

Miriam raised a brow as she tied off the bandage. "You thought I wasn't?"

He gave a sheepish shrug. "Not exactly. I guess I saw you as someone I had to protect."

She sat back on her heels. "I don't think strength is about being fearless. It's about moving forward even when you're scared."

He nodded slowly, allowing the words to settle within him.

"You think you can make it to camp?" she asked, standing and brushing dirt from her skirt. She offered him a hand.

He hesitated for a beat, then took it. Her grip was firm and warm.

"*Jah.*"

They started down the trail together, moving slower than usual, his ankle reminding him of every uneven patch of ground. Iona had gone on ahead to set up camp as Miriam took the lead, navigating the rocks and narrow bends with that quiet grace of hers. He watched the sway of her shoulders, the confidence in her steps. She wasn't hesitant anymore.

"You know," he casually adjusted his pack, "I used to think two people had to lean on each other because one of them would always be stronger. Like… someone had to do the holding up."

Miriam glanced back at him, amused. "And now?"

He gave a half-smile. "Now I think maybe the best ones… the right ones, they take turns."

She didn't answer right away. Just kept walking, the late sun bouncing off her dingy *kapp*.

"I like that."

They were quiet again for a while, but MJ's thoughts ran steady. He hadn't known what kind of woman he'd end up with, if he ever did, but somewhere deep down, he'd always imagined someone like her. Someone who let him be strong but didn't need him to be. Someone soft enough for him to care for, but strong enough to shoulder the hard things when he couldn't.

Someone like Miriam.

By THE TIME they reached camp, the sky was slipping into dusk. The detour had taken longer than expected, and MJ's ankle still ached, but Miriam had been steady and calm the whole way. When they dropped their packs near a small clearing, Iona motioned MJ toward a flat stump near the fire ring.

"Off that foot, now," she swatted the air playfully with her walking stick. "You've done enough limping for one day."

He grumbled something about being perfectly fine, but obeyed.

Miriam had already started pulling out the tent gear as MJ watched her quietly, noting again how strong she had become, both physically and mentally.

Once camp was set and their simple supper warmed by the fire, the three of them sat down with warm mugs and tired limbs. The fire cracked, and cicadas buzzed in the distance.

"You know, that detour today reminded me of something."

MJ glanced at Iona. "Does everything remind you of something?"

"At my age, you've lived enough stories that most things do."

Miriam chuckled and asked, "What did it remind you of?"

Iona poked the fire with a stick. "Of the path I thought my life would take. I always pictured a house full of children. I prayed for them, waited for them, hoped. But they never came."

She paused, letting the silence stretch just enough to be meaningful but not heavy. "For a long time, I thought that meant something was wrong with me. That maybe I had taken the wrong path somewhere, missed a turn. But over time, God made it clear... He didn't forget me. He just gave me a different trail to walk."

Miriam's gaze dropped to her lap. "My *mamm* thinks I shouldn't have children."

Iona looked over, gentle and firm all at once. "You know, people speak all kinds of things over our lives. Sometimes, they mean well, and sometimes, they're just afraid. But their words don't shape your future unless you let them. God's the only one with that kind of power." She leaned closer. "Speak what you believe. What you hope for. Not what you fear."

Miriam looked into the fire, her eyes shining. "I do want children. A home. A purpose. A family."

"And if that's the path He has for you, he'll give you the strength to walk it. Just like He gave you the strength to walk this trail."

MJ shifted beside the fire, his eyes settling on Miriam.

Iona grinned and added, "I think people are like hikers. We don't always choose the terrain. Sometimes, the path gets muddy or washed out, and we end up on a detour. But that doesn't mean it's the wrong way."

She paused, tapping her chest. "Sometimes, the detour is the point. Especially if you're walking it together."

MJ looked at Miriam and then really looked. The quiet around them thickened as if the woods themselves were listening. Her face was soft in the firelight, her eyes steady. He didn't speak, just watched her take in each of Iona's wise words.

CHAPTER 14

*T*he hollow thud of MJ's boots echoed against the wooden planks of the suspension bridge. His ankle felt better that morning as he looked down, the dry ravine stretched out with its walls jagged and steep, shadows pooling at the bottom where the sun couldn't quite reach. The bridge swayed a little with each of his steps. Miriam had already crossed, her figure steady and confident as she waited beneath a canopy of pines on the other side, talking with Iona.

MJ paused halfway across and gripped the side ropes and looked out over the vast wilderness. A hawk wheeled above, its cry sharp and distant. The air here smelled clean and free from the outside world.

Four days on the trail had done something to him, something he hadn't expected. He'd come here to escape his father's expectations and the strain of decisions he wasn't ready to make.

But as the silence of the woods wrapped around him day after day, and his boots kept rhythm with the beat of the trail, something began to shift.

He had told himself for so long that leaving was the answer. That the only way to find freedom was to break away. But out here, with only the trees and sky and Miriam's quiet presence, the need to run had begun to dissolve.

He wasn't sure when it happened. Maybe it was when he saw Miriam smile after conquering a steep incline she hadn't thought she could manage. Or when Iona told a story around the fire that reminded him of how faith could be quiet and personal, not just a list of rules written in the *Ordnung*. Or maybe it was this moment, he thought. *It was never about running.*

It was about becoming a man.

He looked toward the far side of the bridge, where Miriam stood with her hiking poles in hand, her face turned toward the light breaking through the trees. She was stronger than he'd ever realized. And braver.

He thought of her family, of the likely worry stirring back in Willow Springs. His own father probably thought he was gone for good. The Troyers no doubt feared the worst. He should feel guilty. Maybe he did, in some way. But something else had risen stronger than guilt. *Responsibility.* Not the kind his father had hammered into him with talk of duty and heritage, but the kind that came from within. The kind that said, *You don't get to walk away just because it's hard. You don't get to love someone quietly and not show up for them when it counts.* That thought made him draw in a breath.

He wasn't sure if Miriam knew how much she'd changed him. How just by being beside her on this trail laughing, struggling, praying, she'd opened up a part of him he'd closed off long ago.

He wasn't sure what came next. Whether he would return to the farm or find another path, but he knew now that the choice had to come from truth, not fear or frustration. And that, whatever the choice was, it would be about more than rebellion or expectation. It would be about what *Gott* called him to do.

~

THEY STOPPED EARLY THAT DAY. Iona had insisted.

"We've earned a long break," she declared as she dropped her pack beside a smooth rock near the creek's edge. "Besides, my knees are threatening to go on strike."

MJ snorted. "Didn't take you for someone who made a fuss so loudly."

"You hush," Iona shot back with a grin. "There's a difference between quitting and having the good sense to sit down before your legs give out."

Miriam, already unlacing her boots, chuckled. Bear Creek sparkled in the afternoon sun as it trickled over the moss-covered stones.

Once the tents were up and dinner was being rehydrated by the fire, they gathered by the creek with hot cups of tea, letting the silence settle in comfortably.

After a while, Iona tilted her head toward the sky and said, "This place reminds me of a story." She took a second to let the sun warm her face before continuing. "My husband used to say something that has stuck with me through many rough patches."

"What was it?" Miriam asked, tucking a stray hair under her *kapp*.

"He said, 'God plants us in the soil of His choosing. And sometimes it's rocky ground so we'll dig our roots deeper.'"

MJ raised a brow. "Sounds like something that belongs on a mug."

"Oh, I think we had one once," Iona laughed. "He believed that no matter where life put us, it was for a reason, especially the hard places."

Miriam's gaze dropped to her hands in her lap. "Did he still believe that even when… when things got hard at the end?"

Iona smiled. "Especially then. Said the roots he planted in love and in faith would carry on long after he was gone. That's why I kept hiking after he died. I thought maybe I'd find some of those roots again. It turns out God wasn't done planting me."

They sat quietly for a moment.

MJ laughed. "I don't know if I'm growing roots or weeds."

"You'll figure it out," she nudged him with her elbow.

Then she turned to both of them. "You know… this whole journey… it might not even be about you."

Miriam looked up. "What do you mean?"

"Well," Iona rubbed a stick between her fingers, "sometimes God moves us not just for our own growth, but for someone else's. Maybe this little adventure is part of someone else's story. Someone who needs you to go so they can grow."

They were quiet again, the breeze rustling the trees above.

"You think it could be my mother?" Miriam asked.

"Could be. Or someone else. But God doesn't waste movement. If He's got you on a path, there's a reason, even if you don't know it yet."

Miriam leaned back on her elbows and looked toward the canopy of branches and sky overhead. Maybe Iona was right.

Maybe the path she was walking wasn't just for her. Maybe it wasn't just for MJ, either. Maybe *Gott* was

169

planting them both, right where they needed to be, even if the ground was rocky and the way uncertain.

～

THE NEXT DAY, the sun hung lower in the sky as they approached the base of another steep incline. Miriam's legs burned with fatigue, and a quiet agitation began to rise in her chest. Her hands, clutching her hiking poles, ached from the hours of use. She didn't complain. Not once.

But MJ noticed the slight tremble in her shoulders, the way her footfalls dragged just a beat longer than they had the day before.

The trail narrowed here, wrapping along the edge of a slope where the ridge dropped off steeply on one side. MJ moved in close behind her, watching her every step.

"You're dragging your right foot a little. You need to lift it more, or you're gonna catch a root."

"I know," she snapped, trying not to let her frustration spill over.

They kept walking until they reached a flat stretch that opened to a view of the ridge ahead. The last stretch of trail, Table Rock, loomed in the distance. The hardest climb of the entire hike.

Miriam stopped, resting her hands on the tops of her poles, her chest rising and falling with effort.

MJ hesitated before speaking. "Tomorrow's gonna be tough."

She shot him a glance. "I know."

He scratched the back of his neck. "I was thinking… maybe you don't need to finish. You've already done so much. You've nothing to prove."

Her head whipped toward him.

MJ quickly added, "I just mean… what we've done

already, it's incredible. You've done more than most people could, especially with—"

"Especially with what?" Her voice rose, brittle and sharp. "Say it."

He stepped back. "I'm not trying to insult you."

"But you think I can't do it."

"That's not what I said."

"You didn't have to." She shook her head, eyes stinging. "You've been waiting for me to fall apart since the first day... you and everyone else."

"That's not fair—"

"*Nee*, what's not fair is you deciding what I'm capable of!"

"You got lost in the dark, Miriam!"

"I know that!" she shouted. "I know exactly what happened, and I'm the one who sat for hours thinking about it. I don't need you to remind me."

MJ's jaw tightened, but he stayed quiet.

Miriam's voice wavered now... she was tired, but she wouldn't let the trail win. "You think I don't know this trail is hard? That every day, every shadow is a risk I'm taking? I wake up wondering if my eyes will betray me more than yesterday. I'm afraid... I'm afraid I might not even see the summit clearly when we get there."

She paused, eyes fixed on the distant ridgeline.

"But I have to try. I have to know I did it. Once."

MJ looked at her, something shifting in his face. "Iona advised us not to speak death over our lives."

Miriam blinked. "What?"

"You said you're afraid you won't be able to see tomorrow. But what if you can? What if you stop thinking about what might go wrong, and start speaking like you believe something better could happen?"

She said nothing, but he stepped closer.

"I get why you're scared," he added tenderly. "But don't let that fear be the loudest voice in your head."

She swallowed hard. "That's easy for you to say."

"*Nee*, it's not," he almost laughed. "I'm scared too. Scared of what happens when we finish this hike and have to go back."

Their eyes met then, both carrying too many questions, too few answers.

"But I do know one thing. You've shown more strength in these woods than I ever have. So if you want to climb that rock… I'll climb it right beside you."

Miriam took a breath. "Then don't ever tell me again I should quit."

He gave a soft nod, his eyes warm. "I won't. Promise."

The tension loosened considerably between them. Without another word, she turned and started walking again toward the final ascent. And MJ followed, one step behind.

EVELYN STOOD in Miriam's bedroom doorway for a long moment, watching dust motes float in the light streaming in from the window, suspended like memories that refused to settle.

Her apron was dusted with flour she hadn't bothered to brush away. The house was too quiet. Bennie had gone to the woodshop. No one was calling for supper. No voices. No laughter. No footsteps on the stairs. Just stillness.

She walked in and sat on Miriam's neatly made bed, smoothing a corner of the quilt they had stitched together years ago, turquoise and burgundy patches forming a starburst pattern in the center. Her fingers traced a seam they'd laughed over when Miriam stitched it too tight and puckered the fabric.

She closed her eyes and let her hand rest there, suddenly unsure what she was feeling. Control had always come easily to her. It had to. With a house full of *kinner* and a farm to run, there was never room for indecision. Her days were built on the reliable rhythm of an Amish family.

But that family had cracked in the silence of the room. She irreversibly heard what she hadn't wanted to admit. She wasn't angry at Miriam. She was afraid.

Afraid of being left behind. Afraid of no longer being needed. Of having no one to care for. No one to teach how to fold laundry just right or how to cook dumplings that didn't fall apart in the broth. No one to scold or comfort or guide toward the steady, well-lit Amish path she had always believed was safest.

Her last child was slipping from her grasp, and she didn't know who she was without a child to mother. She bowed her head and whispered into the stillness, "*What now, Lord?*"

The silence that followed wasn't empty.

Evelyn drew in a breath that trembled on the way out and looked around the room with new eyes. It still smelled faintly like lavender and cedar, like Miriam's favorite lotion and the wooden dresser Bennie built with his own hands. The life her daughter had lived here was stitched into every piece of fabric and every memory. But it wasn't hers to hold on to anymore.

Her eyes landed on the quilt again, gripping it as if it could tether her to the season slipping away. But even quilts fray. Even mothers must learn when to let go… not from indifference, but from love.

"I only ever wanted her safe and to know she'll be cared for when I'm gone," she whispered to no one, to *Gott* perhaps. "But maybe… maybe safety isn't what she needs right now." A tear slipped down her cheek, quiet and unannounced. And for the first time, Evelyn didn't wipe it away.

~

THE SOFT SOUND of sandpaper against wood was usually enough to clear Bennie's thoughts, but today, his mind wouldn't settle. He ran the paper over the pine table again and again, smoothing the corners into soft curves. A half-drunk mug of black coffee sat cooling on the workbench, untouched for over an hour.

The table was a special order for the bishop. He should've been focused, double-checking measurements or oiling the grain, but all he could think about was Evelyn. She hadn't been herself since Miriam left.

He paused, brushing wood dust from the surface with the side of his hand. It wasn't just that Miriam was gone; it was how quiet Evelyn had become. Her voice no longer carried through the house with instructions or reminders. Her eyes didn't spark the way they used to, not even in frustration. It was like someone had turned down the wick of her spirit.

He wasn't worried about Miriam, not in the way his *fraa* was. He missed her, *jah*. But he knew in his bones that their girl was finding her footing, and when she did, she'd come back. He'd prayed about it every night and that morning, too, right after feeding the calves. Not desperate prayers of pleading, but prayers of thanksgiving, spoken with quiet assurance.

Thank You, Lord, for guiding her. Thank You for watching over her. Thank You for bringing her back in Your time.

A gust of early evening wind stirred in the shop's open

window. Bennie adjusted the table on its side and was reaching for a finer grit of sandpaper when the workshop door creaked open.

"*Ach*, there you are," came the familiar voice of Henry Schrock, the bishop. He ducked his head through the doorway and stepped inside, removing his hat and brushing off the faintest dusting of road grit from his coat. "Thought I'd stop in and check on our table."

Bennie offered him a tired smile. "It's almost ready. Just sanding down the edges."

Henry ran a hand along the smooth top. "Beautiful work, as always."

Bennie nodded, then hesitated.

The bishop glanced at him sideways. "Something on your mind?"

Bennie set the sandpaper down leisurely. "Miriam's been gone more than a week now."

Henry's hand stilled. "Gone where?"

"We don't know exactly," Bennie admitted. "She left after a hard conversation with Evelyn. I think she might be with MJ King. That's my prayer anyway. Evelyn thinks the worst, of course, but MJ is a *goot* boy, and I'm sure she is safe with him."

Henry's eyebrows lifted, but he didn't interrupt.

Bennie exhaled, leaning a hip against the workbench. "I haven't told anyone else, not yet. No need to alarm folks. I just… I believe she needs this time to figure things out. And I trust the Lord to walk with her wherever she's gone."

"You think she ran?" Henry asked.

"*Nee*, I think she left because she needed to breathe. And I believe Evelyn ultimately pushed her too far."

Henry didn't respond right away. He pulled a stool over and sat across from Bennie, resting his hands on his knees.

"I've seen it before. Fear dressing up as love. It convinces us we're protecting our family when we're really trying to control what was never ours to begin with."

Bennie looked down at his hands. "Evelyn doesn't see that. She thinks she'll lose everything if she doesn't hold tight."

Henry nodded. "And what do you think?"

"I think if she keeps holdin' too tight, she'll lose Miriam anyway. I just don't know how to help her let go."

Silence settled between them for a moment. The smell of pine and sawdust clung to the air.

"You know, sometimes the best way to help someone find peace is to live it in front of them. Keep praying. Keep thanking. Keep trusting. But faith... faith grows in stillness."

Bennie nodded. "*Gott* will bring her back," he said again, more to himself than to Henry.

Henry stood and placed a firm hand on Bennie's shoulder. "And He'll bring Evelyn through this, too."

CHAPTER 15

The early morning mist clung to the trees, soft and silver-like. Their boots crunched over damp leaves as they moved around camp, packing up slowly, each in their own thoughts. The final stretch of the Foothills Trail loomed ahead, just a few miles, but it was the most challenging leg, a steady climb toward the summit at Table Rock.

Iona sat on a flat rock near the fire pit, stretching her leg out with a wince. She waved off MJ's concerned look with a small shake of her head and a tired smile.

"It's nothin' I haven't dealt with before." She patted her knee. "This old joint's just barkin' louder than usual."

Miriam dropped into a crouch beside her, worry etched in the shadows beneath her eyes. "You sure you don't want to try it?"

Iona gave her a gentle look, tucking a loose strand of hair under her bandana. "Honey, I've seen the view before. You haven't. And I think this last stretch, it's meant for the two of you."

MJ hesitated, glancing up the trail that wound out of

the trees and disappeared into the slope above. "It doesn't feel right to leave you behind."

Iona chuckled. "I've made my peace with sitting in the sunshine and sipping my tea while you two go make memories. Besides," she leaned forward, her voice softening, "I have a feeling you'll need that time alone more than you know."

Miriam looked at her, uncertain. "What do you mean?"

Iona smiled. "Every trail has a moment where you look back and a moment where you look ahead. That last stretch up there? That's both."

She reached out and squeezed Miriam's hand. "Take it. Climb it. Sit at the top and just… be still. Let your heart settle."

With packs secured and water bottles filled, MJ and Miriam stood at the edge of the trailhead while Iona settled herself on a folding stool beneath a shady pine, her journal and tea at her side.

Miriam adjusted her poles and looked up the trail. "It's steeper than I thought it'd be."

"You don't have to do this."

Miriam smiled. "I do."

They walked in silence for the first ten minutes, the path narrowing and weaving between boulders and gnarled roots. Miriam's breath came in shallow bursts, but she didn't complain. MJ kept a few paces behind her, watching her footing, ready to react should she stumble.

"Do you remember our first hike?" she glanced over her shoulder.

"The pasture loop behind your barn?" he chuckled. "You brought carrot sticks and a stack of books."

"I was twelve," she grinned. "And you kept asking if it was almost over."

"I thought we were lost," he muttered.

Miriam giggled. "Back then, I never imagined a day like this." They kept climbing.

Eventually, the woods thinned, and the light grew clearer. The wind shifted, cooler and stronger as it swept up from the valley below. MJ placed a hand on a mossy boulder and waited while Miriam steadied herself for the final push.

"We're almost there."

She nodded. Her hands were shaking slightly from the effort, but her face was calm.

With one last surge, they emerged onto the overlook, Table Rock stretching beneath them like a patchwork quilt of treetops and stone, fading into the distant blue of the horizon. Neither of them spoke. They simply stood there, side by side, letting the silence settle over them.

Miriam stepped forward, her boots steady on the packed dirt, her heart thudding with more than exertion. Wind tugged at the loose strands of hair around her face. Her skirt clung to her calves, damp with trail dust and dew.

She turned toward MJ, breathless, not from the hike, but from the clarity that was rising inside.

"I didn't think I could do this. Not just the climb. All of it. Leaving. Hiking. Believing I was meant for something more than what others decided for me."

MJ took in a long breath and added, "But you did it."

She nodded, a small smile curling on her lips. "*Jah*. I did."

He was quiet for a long moment. Then, he looked out across the hills. "I've spent so long trying to decide if I belong in the Amish life. Always looking at it like it was something to escape. Like it had to be one thing or the other, freedom or faith."

He turned toward her. "But watching you walk ahead

of me today, sure-footed, stubborn... steady. I saw it differently. You're living this life in a way that looks a lot like freedom."

She met his eyes, heart fluttering.

MJ reached for Miriam's hand, a bold move for someone raised to keep such things reserved, but at that moment, he didn't care about rules or expectations. He needed to anchor her to the moment, to the array of questions looming ahead.

"Come on," he gently tugged her toward a wide, flat ledge overlooking the valley. "Sit with me a while."

Miriam let him lead her, settling beside him as they both stared out over the edge of the world.

He released her hand and asked, "Is there something else you want to see? We could head further south if you want. We don't have to go home if you're not ready."

Miriam didn't answer right away. She wrapped her arms around her knees and gazed out over the horizon. "I think..." she began softly, "I think I'm ready to go home."

MJ blinked, surprised. "Really?"

She nodded. "I've seen more than I ever thought I would. And I now know I can do more than people think. But I also miss my bed, my father's calm, and even Hannah's teasing. If you still want to go on, I can catch a bus home."

He didn't answer immediately. The silence stretched between them, full of thoughts neither of them had spoken aloud. Decisively, he exhaled slowly, rubbing his palms along the tops of his thighs.

"I've been thinking a lot." His voice was rougher now, as if the words were hard to speak. "When I left, I thought I just needed to get away. But out here... I've had time to hear my own thoughts for once. And I think I'm ready. To go home, to take over the farm, to be baptized into the church."

Miriam turned to him, a slow smile forming on her lips. "Are you sure?"

"*Nee*, but I know it's the right next step. And sometimes, that's enough."

They sat in silence for another beat before he added, "So... you're not going back to marry Eli, then?"

She scoffed, the sound light and disbelieving. "That was never going to happen."

He glanced sideways at her. "*Goot.*"

Her cheeks flushed again, but this time it wasn't from the sun. "I do hope I find someone eventually," she admitted. "Someone who doesn't mind a little adventure now and then."

MJ looked back out at the view. "Well, if there's a day when that someone might be me, I'd want to make sure I've got something real to offer. A future. A home. A faith strong enough to carry us both."

She didn't respond immediately, but her smile said more than words could. She leaned into him so their shoulders met. "But you can't stay just for me."

His brow furrowed slightly as she continued.

"You have to stay because you're *called* to. Because you believe this life, this path of tradition and submission, is what *Gott* wants from *you*. Not because of me. Because of Him."

He looked away for a moment, measuring her words.

"If you stay only to build a life with me, it won't be enough when storms come. It has to be more. It has to be His voice that keeps you steady, not mine."

MJ's eyes met hers again, this time with something humbler behind them. "You're right. I think... I finally hear Him." He paused for a few seconds and asked, "Do you want a family someday?"

"I do. Whatever that looks like. However, *Gott* gives it." Then, without thinking, MJ reached for her hand again. It wasn't bold. It wasn't dramatic. Just a brush of fingers against hers, a gentle clasp between calloused hands, quick, respectful, and deeply un-Amish. But for Miriam, it was everything.

He held it only a breath longer than necessary, then released it, his thumb grazing her knuckles as he let go.

Her heart lifted, swelling with something deeper than affection. It was reverence. Not just for him, but for the goodness she saw blooming in him. For the courage it took to stay.

She stood with him, steadied by more than just her feet. Together, they turned back toward the path, toward home, whatever that would mean in the days to come.

THE LATE AFTERNOON sun peaked through the pine trees and across the hood of Iona's dust-covered SUV. Miriam stood beside the open back door as MJ placed Iona's hiking gear inside.

They had returned full circle, back to where their journey had begun. Only now, the road ahead looked entirely different.

Miriam swallowed the lump in her throat as she turned to Iona. "I don't even know how to thank you. You didn't have to help us the way you did."

Iona smiled. "Some things, we're just meant to do. I don't believe in chance meetings. I believe in divine appointments."

MJ stepped forward, offering his hand, that same

Englisch habit that once felt so odd to him. Iona shook it firmly and then pulled him into a quick side hug, bumping her shoulder against his. "Look after her. But more than that, take care of you. Don't forget to figure out what it is you were created to do, not just what's expected of you."

MJ gave a small, grateful nod. "*Jah.*"

Turning back to Miriam, Iona reached out and brushed a bit of leaf from her sweater. "God planted you deep, sweetheart. You're going to grow tall… but don't be afraid to let Him prune what doesn't belong. Even the good things sometimes have to go to make room for the best."

Miriam blinked fast. "Will we see you again?"

"Maybe." Iona's grin turned wistful. "But some people come into your life for just a season. This—" she gestured around the wooded lot, the air thick with memory and meaning— "this was our season. And it was a good one."

She reached into her coat pocket and pulled out a small, dog-eared notebook. "Here." She placed it in Miriam's hand. "My favorite trail scriptures. Notes I've scribbled over the years. Use them. Add your own. One day, you'll pass it on."

Miriam clutched the notebook to her chest.

"Remember," Iona added as she stepped into her driver's seat, "words hold power. Speak life, not fear. Promise me that."

"I promise," Miriam whispered.

As Iona pulled away, dust trailing behind her, MJ and Miriam stood silently together. The SUV disappeared around the bend, leaving only stillness and the scent of pine.

Miriam looked down at the notebook in her hand, its pages fluttering in the breeze.

"She was right," she murmured. "This really was our season, even though it was but a short one."

MJ smiled and replied. "I don't think it's over yet."

～

EVELYN STEPPED out onto the porch, her shawl wrapped tightly around her shoulders. The birds had already begun their spring chorus, but to her ears, the world was strangely quiet. Hollow, almost.

Each day, since Miriam had vanished, had started this way: with hope held loosely in her chest, like a bird too tired to fly.

She didn't say a word to Bennie as she passed him in the yard. He was heading to the woodshop, whistling low, as he always did, when trying not to worry. She didn't stop at the chicken coop to gather eggs or the washhouse. Today, she made a straight line for the phone shanty at the end of the lane.

She opened the door, and the scent of dust reached her nose; the silence was nearly suffocating. Evelyn reached out with steady fingers and checked the answering machine, not really expecting anything. But then... *one new message.*

She stared at the blinking light like it might vanish if she looked away. She pressed the button, heart thudding so hard it echoed in her ears.

Miriam's voice filled the small space.

"*Mamm. Datt.*" Her voice was quiet, a little shaky, but steady enough. "I—I just wanted to call and let you know I'm okay. I'm with MJ, and we're heading home. We've been hiking... seeing some things. I know I should've told you before I left, and I'm sorry. I didn't mean to worry you. I just needed... space. I needed to think. I needed to see what I was capable of." There was a short pause, a soft sigh.

"When I get back, I'd like to sit down with you both. I want to talk about the future. About what I'm hoping for and how I want to live… the life *Gott's* given me. I'm not trying to go against your wishes. I just need you to trust me. I'm not a child anymore." Another pause. "We'll be home in a few days." *Click.*

The machine beeped again, signaling the end of the message. Evelyn stood frozen, one hand pressed to her chest. The relief came fast and thick, so fierce it knocked the breath from her lungs. But beneath it, something else stirred. *Guilt.*

She had feared losing her daughter. But in trying to control her, had she driven her away?

Evelyn closed her eyes and whispered, "Thank You, Lord."

Then she turned and walked slowly back toward the house, one step at a time, not as the woman who always had the answers, but as a mother, ready to finally listen.

Miriam handed MJ his phone back, and he stared at it a moment longer before sliding it into his coat pocket. She had left the message without faltering. It struck him how different she seemed from the girl who once tiptoed around her mother's moods.

"That was brave."

Miriam gave a little shrug. "It was time."

They sat in the stillness of the parked truck for a few moments before Miriam turned her head toward him. "Would you mind seeing one more thing before we go home?"

He raised a brow. "That depends."

"How far are we from the ocean?"

His brows shot up. "The ocean?"

Miriam gave a sheepish smile. "I've never seen it. And... if I don't see it now, I may never get another chance."

He didn't tease her. Didn't even smile. He simply reached for his phone, tapped a few times, and nodded. "Five hours east. Atlantic coast. We could be there before sunset."

Miriam beamed, her eyes bright with anticipation. "Really?"

MJ turned the engine over. "Really!"

THE ROAD STRETCHED out for hours, pine trees lining both sides, and long patches of sun filtering through the windshield. MJ drove with one hand on the wheel, the other resting loosely on his leg. Beside him, Miriam was uncharacteristically quiet, her face turned toward the window, eyes trailing the blur of trees. They had left Table Rock behind, but neither of them could shake the shadow of what waited back home.

After a few minutes of quiet, Miriam spoke again, her voice softer now. "I'm not sure how my mother will take it. Me standing up for myself like this. Telling her I want to make my own decisions."

"She'll come around," MJ didn't sound convinced.

Miriam gave a small, tired laugh. "You don't know her."

"I know what it's like to carry someone else's expectations. My *datt*, he always assumed I'd be like my brothers. Take over the farm. But I don't want it, never have. I like the Feed & Seed," he continued. "Working with people, ordering inventory, knowing what the community needs, it makes sense to me. I've even considered converting our old barn into a soybean drying facility. It'd serve the whole district. Something useful. Something different."

"That actually sounds... perfect. You're still helping people. Just in a new way."

He shrugged. "Don't know if my *datt* would ever go for it. But I think I'm done letting that stop me."

She smiled, a quiet pride blooming in her chest. "I'm glad."

Then he glanced at her again. "What about you? What do you want?"

She took a long breath, her fingers twisting in the fabric of her skirt. "I want to do something that matters. Maybe in a store like that. Helping people. I can still do a lot of things, even if I can't see everything clearly."

MJ started to speak, but she raised her hand, stopping him.

"I know it might get worse. But I'm not going to sit around waiting for that day. Maybe I'll need help reading fine print someday, but there will always be something I can do. I'm not letting this"—she tapped her temple lightly—"Be the thing that defines the rest of my life."

He looked at her for a long moment. "You're stronger than you think."

Miriam smiled as the cab fell quiet again, the silence no longer strained but steady, at ease.

THEY PULLED into a gravel parking lot just off the main road, the sign reading Public Beach Access – Myrtle

Beach. MJ shut off the engine and leaned forward over the steering wheel, taking in the stretch of coastline just beyond the sand dunes. The sea breeze immediately found its way into the cracked window, carrying with it the sharp scent of salt and the faint echo of waves breaking against the shore.

Miriam sat silently beside him, her eyes wide with curiosity as she stared past the weathered boardwalk. People bustled across the lot, some in sandals, others barefoot, a few in light jackets.

"I didn't think so many people would be here."

"Me neither, but it's the ocean… guess we're not the only ones drawn to it."

They got out and slipped off their shoes, carrying them by the heels as they made their way down the sandy path. The sand squeezed between their toes as the waves came into view and Miriam stopped in her tracks.

The sound alone made her smile, but it was the sight of the blue horizon, the glittering sun dancing on the water, and the foamy whitecaps stretching out like a living painting that pulled a breathless laugh from her throat.

Without a word, she took off running.

"Miriam!" MJ called after her, but he couldn't help the grin that broke across his face.

She kicked up sand as she raced barefoot toward the waves, her dress billowing behind her and her arms stretched out like wings. When the tide rushed in and kissed her toes, she let out a squeal and jumped back, only to chase the next wave in. Her laughter rang out, free and unguarded, catching on the wind like a hymn.

MJ stood still, watching her intently. It was at that moment that he knew, without a doubt, she was the one he wanted to walk through life with.

They sat side by side in the sand, shoes tucked behind

them, the ocean stretching out like an endless quilt stitched by *Gott's* own hand. The wind had picked up, a soft chill threading through the early evening breeze. Miriam tugged her sweater close and leaned back on her hands, tilting her face toward the sun with her eyes closed.

"I want to remember this. The warmth on my face... the sound of the waves. On one of those bitter January mornings when the snow's piled high and the wind won't quit howling through the barn, I want to pull this memory out like a piece of hard candy. Let it linger in my mind."

He didn't answer right away. His hands were clasped loosely over his knees. "Miriam," he stretched out the silence, "once we're back... and I've sorted some things out, I was wonderin' if maybe you'd consider steppin' out with me."

She turned toward him, surprised by the gentle weight of his words. "*Jah.*"

He looked at her then, his gaze steady, his voice low. "I know things aren't simple between us. But once I talk to the bishop, and I settle where I stand in the church... well, I'd like to get to know you better. Proper-like."

Miriam looked back toward the waves, a soft laugh escaping her lips. "You think the bishop's going to look kindly on me? After I ran off with an unbaptized man and crossed state lines without a chaperone?"

MJ's mouth twitched. "Well, when you say it like that..."

She gave him a sidelong glance, her smile fading into something more serious. "Truth is, I'm not just worried about my parents or the bishop. What worries me more is what the road ahead looks like."

He nodded, waiting.

"The doctor says I won't go completely blind, but the center of my vision, it'll never be clear. Fine print, sewing, reading books, all of it is fading. There might come a time when I can't be much help the way someone expects a woman to be. I don't want to be a burden to anyone."

He was quiet, letting the words settle between them like tidewater smoothing the sand.

"When two folks care for one another, and I'm not saying too much here, just being honest, what comes down the road, they face together. Not apart. Not hiding from it."

She turned to look at him again as he added, "My *datt* always says marriage is less about what two people can do *for* each other, and more about what they can carry *with* each other. I reckon he's right about that."

Miriam blinked hard, the sea breeze tugging lightly at the loose strands of her hair. "You sound more like a baptized member every day."

He smiled. "Maybe I'm finally listening to what I should've heard all along."

They fell into a quiet rhythm, just the sound of the waves and the occasional cry of a gull overhead. MJ reached down and drew a line in the sand with his finger.

"This ocean. It's big. And it's wild. But sittin' here with you, it doesn't feel half as uncertain as the road back home used to."

Miriam didn't say anything, but she moved just slightly closer, the sleeve of her sweater brushing his arm. It wasn't a confession. It wasn't a promise. But it was enough.

CHAPTER 16

The house was quiet when Miriam stepped through the back door, her boots leaving soft prints on the mat as she paused, listening. She half-expected a storm of questions, a flood of scolding words, but the kitchen was still. Only the soft bubbling of the kettle on the stove and the smell of baking molasses cookies filled the space.

Her mother was at the counter, her back to the door, hands deliberately folding a dish towel. For a moment, she didn't turn. Miriam stood in the doorway, taking in the familiar sight of her mother, her ever-tidy starched *kapp*, the slope of her shoulders, the apron tied with careful precision. This was the woman who had stitched her dresses, taught her to knead dough, and scolded her for muddy hems and overcooked noodles. This was the woman who had been her whole world once, but now was someone she had to explain herself to.

Evelyn finally turned, her expression unreadable. Her eyes landed on Miriam and stayed there. No greeting, no embrace. Only the quiet acknowledgment of her daughter's return.

"You're home," her voice cool but calm.

"*Jah*," Miriam replied, her own voice soft.

For a few moments, neither said anything. The kettle began to hiss, and Evelyn turned away to tend to it. She reached for the loose-leaf tea tin, the one reserved for special days, and spooned fragrant chamomile into the strainer before pouring the steaming water over it. She added just the right amount of honey to the cup, the way Miriam liked it.

She placed the mug gently on the table. "Your favorite."

Miriam's heart twisted at the gesture. She moved to the table, slid into the seat, and wrapped her hands around the warm cup. "*Denki*," she whispered.

Her mother sat down across from her, folding her hands in her lap. Her eyes, always sharp and knowing, studied Miriam carefully. "You were gone a long time."

Miriam nodded. "I know."

"People have been talking."

"I know that, too."

"You've been traveling with MJ?"

Miriam took a breath and met her mother's eyes. "*Jah*."

Miriam set the mug down and folded her hands on the table. Her voice was steady but full of emotion. "*Mamm*... I'm not marrying Eli Shetler."

Evelyn's mouth opened slightly as if to respond, but Miriam held up her hand. "Please. Let me finish."

The older woman closed her lips but narrowed her eyes, bracing herself.

"I know you think you're doing what's best for me," she

continued. "I know you're scared. And I understand why. You've watched me struggle. You've seen the way my sight has changed, how uncertain my future might be." She paused, searching for the right words. "But *Mamm*... that's fear. It's not love. It's not trust. You've been trying to protect me so fiercely that you've built a wall around me. One I can't breathe behind."

Evelyn blinked but didn't look away.

"I want to be a mother someday," Miriam's voice cracked now. "And a wife. A good one. A faithful one. But only if I truly love the man I marry. Only if I believe he was placed in my path by *Gott*, not by someone else's fear."

Evelyn's jaw tightened. "And is that someone MJ?"

There was an edge to her voice now, bitterness, maybe even disappointment.

Miriam didn't flinch. "I don't know yet." She was quiet for a moment. "We didn't plan any of this. And we didn't do anything improper. MJ was... respectful. Protective. Kind. He honored my feelings in ways I didn't even expect."

"You were alone together," her mother snapped. "For days. What do you think the bishop will say when he hears of that?"

Miriam's eyes flashed, but her voice stayed calm. "Whatever he says, I will face him myself. This is my life, *Mamm*. Not yours to explain or defend."

Evelyn looked away then, out the window over the sink. "You were always the dreamer," she murmured. "Always with your head in the clouds."

"*Mamm*... you need to understand something. I don't want to fight you. I don't want to walk away. I want to stay. I want to raise my *kinner* here someday. I want to be part of the community. But I need the space to grow into the woman *Gott* is calling me to be, not the woman *you* think I should become."

Her voice trembled, but she held firm. "Please don't speak fear over my life anymore. I know my diagnosis is hard to face. But you've spoken so many harsh words about my future, you've made me feel broken before anything has even happened."

Her mother's eyes filled with tears, and she looked away quickly, pretending to brush something from the corner of her eye.

"I don't want your fear to be the voice I carry into my future. I want to carry hope. And faith. And the belief that no matter what happens, *Gott* will give me what I need."

Silence filled the kitchen again. The ticking of the wall clock sounded unusually loud.

Finally, Evelyn rose from her chair. She walked over to the counter, her back once again to Miriam. "I was just trying to protect you."

"I know. But now I need you to trust me."

For a long moment, her mother stood still. Then, she turned around slowly. Her eyes were red, her face weary.

"I don't know if I can," she said honestly.

Miriam nodded. "That's okay. Maybe one day you will."

She stood and picked up her tea. As she turned to leave the kitchen, she paused beside her mother.

"I still need you, *Mamm.* Just not the way I used to." And then she walked out, leaving Evelyn standing in the quiet, the scent of chamomile still hanging in the air.

THE TICKING clock in the corner marked the only sound in the room. Evelyn sat in her favorite rocker near the window, the one that overlooked the front yard and the lane beyond. The moon spilled through the front window and over the wooden floor.

Her hands, still rough from years of work, rested in her lap, empty now, for once. No mending. No knitting. No busywork to distract her. Only the stillness and a quiet ache deep inside.

She looked toward the stairs where Miriam had gone to bed hours ago. The house sat heavier than it had in a long time, not with sadness, but with change.

She hadn't expected her daughter's voice to be so steady. Or her words to land so true. It had stunned her to be on the receiving end of strength that had once needed her guidance to grow.

But she had seen it. Not a flicker of rebellion, but something far deeper. A settled strength. A grounded peace.

She pressed her fingers to her lips, remembering how many times she had spoken too quickly. Too sharply. How often her words had shaped the air in this house, sometimes like walls, sometimes like weapons.

Miriam hadn't thrown them back at her. She had only stood firm in her beliefs. And now she had seen Miriam differently, not as a girl struggling against the current, but as a woman who had chosen to plant her feet in the stream and face it head-on.

"I was wrong," she whispered aloud, as if the walls needed to hear it too. "I've treated her diagnosis like a chain. Something to manage. Something to control." But it wasn't. It was simply part of her testimony.

"She's still whole," she whispered. "Even if her eyes fail... she's not broken."

The thought rose unexpectedly, like a breath of wind through a closed door. It surprised her with its clarity.

"I thought I was the strong one," she muttered to herself. "But she has a strength I never taught her. A strength that didn't come from me at all."

She turned her eyes toward the moon outside, bright against the night sky.

"*Maybe that's the point,*" she thought. "*Maybe all these years, I've been trying to be her answer… and all along, Gott was shaping her for something I couldn't see.*"

She didn't cry. The tears had come and gone over the last couple of weeks, worn out and wrung dry. This was different. This was a settling. A silent vow.

She would try, from here on out, to speak life instead of death. She would try to see what *Gott* saw… an inner strength in her youngest daughter that could only come from the peace she found in the Lord.

MJ STOOD by the split-rail fence, his old pickup truck idling for the last time in his ownership. His *Englisch* friend, Tom, clutched the steering wheel with a tentative smile. MJ took a steadying breath and reached through the open window to shake Tom's hand. "Take good care of her, *jah?*" MJ patted the dusty blue hood of the truck. Tom nodded, understanding the weight of the moment. They both knew this was more than just a vehicle sale, it was MJ saying goodbye to a piece of the life he'd lived outside the Amish way.

MJ's chest tightened, and he swallowed against the lump in his throat. The old truck had been freedom on four wheels; countless summer evenings driving on country roads, laughing with friends, windows down, and *Englisch* music playing.

Now, it rattled off in the distance, stirring up a trail of

dust that lingered in the still air before slowly settling back to earth. In the quiet that followed, he became aware of the gentle sounds of home: the clip-clop of a buggy horse stomping in the barn, crickets beginning their dusk chorus in the fields, and the wind rustling through the open barn door.

The *Englisch* world grew distant with every second, and in its place remained the familiar serenity of Amish country. Bittersweet as it was, a strange peace washed over MJ as the noise of the truck faded away. One chapter of his life had closed, and another was waiting to begin.

He turned and made his way back toward the farmhouse. On the front porch, his father stood waiting in his plain dark broadcloth trousers, thumbs tucked into his suspenders. The older man's beard caught the light of sunset as he gazed out at the road where the truck had vanished.

MJ approached slowly; he half-expected an awkward silence, so much had been said... and yelled on this porch in the past about that forbidden truck. But tonight, there was no anger in his father's face, only a gentle, studying expression.

"*Es ist fertig?*" his father asked quietly. No judgment in the question, only concern for his son.

MJ managed a small smile. "*Jah, Datt,* it is done."

He stepped up onto the porch, removing his straw hat and running a hand through his hair. The last rays of the sun warmed his back, and he realized his palms trembled slightly, not from regret, but from the enormity of what he needed to say next. He had come back not just to the farm but to the faith and family he'd nearly left behind. Now was the moment to reveal the truth to his father.

His father motioned to the wooden bench swing, and they both sat down. The bench creaked under their weight, swaying ever so lightly. For a long moment, neither spoke. A distant cow lowed from the barn, and a barn cat slipped across the porch steps, winding around MJ's legs. He inhaled the familiar scent of wood smoke from the kitchen stove. This was home, and he needed to reclaim it with honesty. He cleared his throat, breaking the stillness.

"*Datt*," he began, voice low. "I need to talk to you, to tell you why I'm doing this." He nodded back in the direction of the road, implying the truck and all it represented. His father remained quiet, eyes attentive beneath his wire-rimmed glasses perched low on his nose, encouraging him to continue. MJ's fingers laced together nervously. "I'm not joining the church because I'm supposed to, or because you and *Mamm* expect it." His words came out steadily, gaining strength. "I'm doing it because… I want to. Because it feels right. I've found peace with who I am, and where I come from."

He paused, gauging his father's reaction. In the growing twilight, it was hard to read all the emotions on his father's weathered face. MJ thought he saw a glimmer of moisture in the older man's eyes, but it might have just been a trick of the soft light. His father drew a breath, and MJ hurried on, needing to explain fully. "When I was out there," he gestured faintly toward the horizon beyond which lay the *Englisch* world; the towns, the endless roads, the life he'd tasted… "I thought I wanted that. The freedom, the music, the machines…" He shook his head. "I fought our way of life for a long time because I didn't want to admit you might have been right." MJ's voice caught, and he let out a shaky chuckle. "I guess I was a little stubborn."

His father finally smiled, and a quiet laugh puffed from his lips like air released from a bellows. "You get that from me," he said tenderly.

Encouraged, MJ continued. "Selling the truck... giving all that up, it isn't a sacrifice now. It's what I want. I want to be part of the community because it's who I am. Not because I have to, but because in my heart, I know it's where I belong." As soon as those words were out, MJ exhaled, a tension unwinding inside him that he hadn't realized was wound so tight. It was the pure truth, finally spoken. He had crossed an invisible bridge in that moment, one built on his own free will. He looked up at his father, feeling unburdened and strangely free.

His father's eyes searched his, and MJ braced himself. He half-expected a reprimand out of habit, perhaps a reminder of the pain his brief rebellion had caused the family or a caution about commitment. But instead, his father's face broke into an expression of profound relief and gentle joy.

"It was never about forcing you to stay. It was about hoping and praying you'd find your way, in your own time." He paused and gathered his thoughts before continuing. "From the day you were born, I asked the Lord to guide your steps. I had to trust that He would speak to your heart when you were ready."

Tears pricked the corners of MJ's eyes. He swallowed hard, keeping them in check. His father's words were like a balm on old wounds of guilt and doubt. All those arguments, the silence at the dinner table, the nights MJ came home late from running around with *Englisch* friends —through it all, his father had been hoping and praying that he would come to *Gott* on his own.

His father had planted the seeds of faith and identity in him since childhood, and though MJ had wandered, those seeds had quietly taken root.

His father cleared his throat and continued, speaking now as if a dam had broken, gently but with years of wisdom pouring out. "We believe that faith is only real when it's chosen freely, willingly. Your mother and I could teach you and guide you… even scold you," he added with a soft chuckle, "but in the end, your choice had to be your own. The Lord doesn't want a reluctant soldier. He wants your heart given freely."

MJ nodded. "I know that now. I'm sorry it took me so long to understand." His voice cracked slightly. "I'm sorry for the worry I caused you and *Mamm*."

His father shook his head, dismissing the apology kindly. "*Nee*, it's all forgiven. What matters is that you're here now."

He reached out and, to MJ's surprise, pulled him into a brief, firm embrace. MJ closed his eyes and sank into that hug, returning it with gratitude. He couldn't remember the last time his father had hugged him. It wasn't common for him to show affection so openly, but in this quiet moment on the porch, the embrace came without hesitation. Father and son, once at odds, now held each other with understanding. The tension of past conflicts melted away.

When they drew apart, his father looked at him with a proud, misty-eyed expression. "You've become a fine man. The Lord has worked in your heart, and it gladdens me to see it."

A smile found its way to MJ's face, and a tear he didn't bother hiding slipped down. It was rare to hear such words from his father, whose humility often kept him from praising anyone too much. MJ realized in that moment how hungry he had been to earn that approval, not by driving a truck or living like the *Englisch*, but by being true to himself and his heritage.

They sat together a while longer on the porch swing, talking about the days to come. His father spoke of the baptism classes MJ would join with the other youth. MJ listened, astonished at how readily his father had opened his arms to him even before MJ had made it official. He realized that despite his worrying, there had always been a place for him here at home.

Finally, their words gave way to a comfortable silence. Fireflies danced in the flowerbeds lining the porch, and the pale moon rose over the fields. MJ's father leaned back, rocking the swing smoothly with one foot. In that peaceful silence, MJ allowed himself to imagine the future... a future here on this very farm, rooted in faith and family. He pictured sitting in this same spot years from now, perhaps with a wife at his side and children playing at his feet, teaching them the same values that meant so much to his father.

Thank you, Lord, MJ prayed silently, his heart full. He understood now what peace truly felt like. It was this: a quiet evening on an Amish farm, the person he respected most by his side, and the sure knowledge that he was exactly where he was meant to be. He was home for good, not out of obligation, but out of love and conviction.

"Come inside, *Mamm* has made a pie." His eyes were bright with contentment as he added with a tender grin. "And I suspect she's eager to hear what you just told me."

MJ chuckled, feeling light as air. As MJ crossed the threshold of the house, he knew he was stepping into a new chapter of his life.

The door closed behind them with a soft thud, and he wished he had explained his dreams for the farm, but that would come at a later time. For now, he had come full circle. Whatever the future held... work, love, children, trials or joys, he would face it firmly planted in the soil of his upbringing, his faith as his guide and his family at his side. And that, he thought, was a future as promising as Miriam's smile that continued to tug at his heart.

∼

THE AIR inside The Mercantile was warm and still, scented with the aroma of deli meat and fresh bread. Miriam stepped lightly through the narrow aisles, her basket looped over her arm, eyes lowered but attentive. She didn't expect to see him, not here, not today, but her heart quickened anyway when she caught sight of him near the barrels of molasses and lamp oil.

MJ looked up at the same moment. Their eyes met, just briefly, and he gave the smallest nod. Respectful. Steady. But behind it, something deeper lingered.

He stepped toward her, careful to keep his voice low and their distance appropriate. "Afternoon, Miriam."

"Afternoon," she replied softly, fingers brushing the hem of her sleeve.

A long beat passed in the quiet, the hum of voices behind the counter filling the space between them.

"I left something for you…" Almost as if he wasn't sure he should. "Out by the creek. The usual spot."

Her eyes flicked up to meet his. "I'll look for it," she whispered, and her voice held more than agreement; it held hope.

He gave the faintest smile, and with it came the memory of every word they'd once written, every book passed in secret, every glance heavy with things unspoken. "It's not much. Just something I needed to say."

She nodded, and for a moment, it was like the world softened around them. A thousand things unsaid, but all understood.

With a final tip of his hat, MJ turned and walked toward the door, his boots making no sound on the wooden floor.

Miriam stood still for a moment, the handle of the

basket firm beneath her fingers. Even though it had been weeks since their adventure, he still had a way of stirring something in her, a quiet excitement for what he might have written, tucked away in their secret world beneath the trees, where life began and ended with awe. A future not yet spoken but already starting to unfold between them.

EPILOGUE

The following year, January 15th

Snow clung softly to the fence rails and the edges of the lane, dressing the path to Miriam's parents' farmhouse in a hush of winter white. Inside, the warmth of lamplight flickered across familiar faces gathered for her birthday supper. It was a modest, simple, sweet celebration, just as she liked it.

Miriam sat at the table, cheeks flushed from the fire's warmth, her heart fuller than it had been in years. A year ago, she'd stepped out into the unknown, unsure of what lay ahead. Now, she sat steady, not without questions, but with peace found in the faces of the people she loved.

Her mother had baked her favorite carrot cake without being asked. A quiet offering. A truce. They were still learning to walk gently around each other, still finding their way back to something new, and that was enough for now.

After the last plate was washed and put away, MJ stood and cleared his throat.

"If it's alright," his eyes flickered from Bennie to Miriam, "I'd like to say something."

Evelyn's hands stilled over the teacups.

"Miriam and I..." MJ began, steady as a well-laid beam. "We've spoken with the bishop. We plan to marry next month if it's the Lord's will."

Silence fell, a stillness like snowfall. Then Bennie's smile broke wide and sure. Hannah clapped her hands softly in joy. Evelyn said nothing for a breath, then gave a small, trembling smile and nodded.

No fanfare, no elaborate words. Just truth. Just the way things ought to be.

Later, as the family lingered in the front room, MJ caught Miriam's eye from across the room and gave her a tilt of his head.

"Go get your boots on. And your coat. I've got something to show you."

She raised a brow. "Out in this cold?"

He shrugged, one corner of his mouth lifting. "It'll be worth it."

Ten minutes later, they were walking the familiar trail behind the farm, the snow quiet underfoot, the sky above washed in lavender dusk. The trees stood tall and bare, every branch etched in silver.

"Almost there."

Rounding a curve near the bend in the path, Miriam stopped short. There, strung between two trees, was a thick guide wire stretched gently forward. Her breath caught. Posts followed every few yards, disappearing into the woods along the trail they'd walked so many times before.

The wire shimmered faintly in the low light, barely visible to anyone else, but to Miriam, it was everything.

Her fingers reached out and brushed it. "You did this?"

"*Jah*, just about a mile's worth. Far enough to feel free... close enough to home."

She turned toward him, her heart swelling with something that had no name.

"I thought," he continued, voice low, "if the day ever came when it got harder to see... you shouldn't have to wait on anyone. I want you to be able to walk this trail on your own."

Her tears came, soft and sure. She didn't brush them away.

"I wanted you to know," MJ added, "you won't ever walk it alone. Not really."

Miriam nodded, the cold air sharp in her lungs, the warmth in her chest undoing her. Snowflakes had begun to fall again, slow and weightless, dotting the trail like scattered blessings. And though no words were spoken, in that quiet place between snow and sky, both of them knew: their paths had nearly missed, but *Gott*, in His perfect timing, had stitched their lives together like the switchbacks of a mountain trail. Twisting, rising, unexpected... and yet always leading home.

What they'd learned on the Foothills Trail wasn't just about endurance or direction. It was about walking beside someone, even when the way was steep, the light was dim, and the future uncertain.

Miriam reached out and rested her fingers on the wire MJ had strung, thick, steady, and sure, guiding her forward when sight might one day fail. A quiet promise wrapped in wood and wire.

She remembered the promise she'd made a year ago: "*To live life fully, no matter what.*" Now, with MJ beside her and the trail ahead aglow with snow, she whispered that promise again, this time not just to herself, but to the One who had led her here: *"I'll keep walking. I'll keep believing. I'll keep trusting. Because I know You'll never stop guiding me on the path that brings You the most glory, just like You led me to this mile, this man, and this moment. Exactly where You meant me to be all along."*

AMISH ROMANCE BIRTHDAY SERIES

Love doesn't follow a calendar... but sometimes, a single month can change everything.

In this special *Amish Romance Birthday Series*, twelve beloved authors invite you to celebrate a year of faith, friendship, and falling in love . . . one month at a time.

Whether it's a promise made in the cold of winter, a prayer whispered in summer, or a dream fulfilled beneath the harvest moon, these twelve tales remind us that every month can be a season of grace.

Twelve months. Twelve stories. One unforgettable year of Amish romance.

Miriam's January Promise by Tracy Fredrychowski - *Lilly's February Love* by Kelly Irvin - *Amelia's March Arrangement* by Mindy Steele - *Arie's April Beginnings* by Rachel J. Good - *Maggie's May Wish* by Diane Craver - *Jolene's June Prayer* by Ashley Emma - *Rose's July Surprise* by Adina Senft - *Annie's August Frolic* by Jennifer Beckstrand - *Tabitha's September Homecoming* by Kathleen Fuller - *Julia's October Blessing* by Jennifer Spredemann - *Mary's November Dream* by Susan Lantz Simpson - *Hannah's December Gift* by Debra Torres

The series continues here: *Amish Romance Birthday Series*

https://www.amazon.com/dp/B0FVT4GCM6

CARROT CAKE

WITH ORANGE GLAZE

Ingredients for the Cake

- 2 cups whole-wheat flour
- 1 cup brown sugar
- 1 cup white sugar
- 2 teaspoons baking powder
- 2 teaspoons baking soda
- 2 teaspoons cinnamon
- 1 teaspoon nutmeg
- 1 teaspoon salt
- 1 ¼ cups vegetable oil
- 1 (12-ounce) can frozen unsweetened orange juice (reserve ¼ of the can for glaze)
- 4 eggs
- 2 ½ cups grated carrots
- ½ cup chopped nuts (walnuts or pecans work well)

Instructions

Preheat oven to 350°F (175°C). Grease and flour a bundt pan. In a large bowl, whisk together the flour, brown sugar, white sugar, baking powder, baking soda, cinnamon, nutmeg, and salt. Add the vegetable oil and ¾ of the can of orange juice (reserving ¼ for the glaze). Mix well. Add eggs one at a time, beating well after each addition. Stir in the grated carrots and chopped nuts until evenly distributed. Pour batter into the prepared pan and bake for 1 hour, or until a toothpick inserted in the center comes out clean. Let the cake cool slightly while preparing the glaze.

Ingredients for the Orange Glaze

- 6 tablespoons butter

- Reserved ¼ can of orange juice
- 2 cups powdered sugar

Instructions

In a small saucepan, melt the butter over medium heat until lightly browned, stirring frequently. Remove from heat and whisk in the reserved orange juice and powdered sugar until smooth. Pour the warm glaze over the cake while it is still warm. Let cool completely before serving. Enjoy!

GLOSSARY

PENNSYLVANIA "DEUTSCH" WORDS

Ausbund. Amish songbook.

bruder. Brother.

denki. Thank You.

doddi. Grandfather.

doddi house. A small house next to the main house.

g'may. Community

goot meiya. Good morning.

jah. Yes.

kapp. Covering or prayer cap.

kinner. Children.

mamm. Mother or mom.

mommi. Grandmother.

nee. No.

Ordnung. Order or set of rules the Amish follow.

rumshpringa. Running-around period.

schwester. Sister.

singeon. Singing/youth gathering.

WHAT DID YOU THINK?

First of all, thank you for purchasing *Miriam's January Promise*. I hope you will enjoy all the books in this series. If you enjoyed this book and found it beneficial, I'd appreciate hearing from you and hope you will take a moment to post a review on Amazon.

https://www.amazon.com/dp/B0FVGF9G97

If you love visiting Willow Springs, I invite you to sign up for my email list and enjoy *Love Blooms at the Apple Blossom Inn*:

https://tracyfredrychowski.com/love-blooms-at-the-apple-blossom-inn/

If you would like to explore a reading order and a complete list of all the books in my collection, please visit: https://tracyfredrychowski.com/books-by-tracy-fredrychowski/

ABOUT THE AUTHOR

Tracy Fredrychowski's life closely mirrors the gentle, simple stories she crafts in her writing. With a passion for the simple side of life, Tracy regularly shares tips on her website and blog at https://tracyfredrychowski.com.

In northwestern Pennsylvania, Tracy grew up steeped in the virtues of country living. A pivotal moment in her life was the tragic murder of a young Amish woman in her community. This event profoundly influenced her, compelling her to dedicate her writing to the peaceful lives of the Amish people. Tracy aims to inspire her readers through her stories to embrace a life centered around faith, family, and community.

For those intrigued by the Amish way of life, Tracy extends an invitation to connect with her on Facebook. On her page, she shares captivating Amish photography by her friend Jim Fisher and recipes, short stories, and glimpses into her cherished Amish community nestled deep in the heart of northwestern Pennsylvania's Amish country.

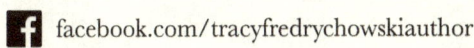 facebook.com/tracyfredrychowskiauthor